# THE SPLIT DECISION

"*The Vegas Knockout* is a funny book, full of engaging characters that cover the spectrum of human likeability. What makes it more than a piece of fluff is how Schreck uses Duffy's love of boxing to stand in for any devotion truly held. Duffy's success is in his journey, just as the greatest fun in *The Vegas Knockout* is in the reading."

— DANA KING, AUTHOR OF THE PENNS RIVER CRIME NOVELS


"*Out Cold* floored me with a quick one-two of the serious and seriously funny. Schreck's unique blending of the absurd and the sublime, along with his rather oddball cast of characters, makes *Out Cold* a great read."

— REED FARREL COLEMAN, TWO-TIME SHAMUS AWARD WINNING AUTHOR OF *EMPTY EVER AFTER*


"*Out Cold* is a fast, funny, rip-roaring read, and Schreck's wit and humor shine through on every page. But what I love most about Schreck's creation, Duffy Dombrowski, is the decency and dignity with which he treats the unforgettable cast of loonies, addicts, and criminals who parade through his office. I haven't cared this much about a protagonist in a good long while. Duffy is a real hero and a true original."

— BLAKE CROUCH, AUTHOR OF *ABANDON*

"Fresh, intense and funny, Schreck's second mystery to feature unrepentant Elvis fan and dog lover Duffy Dombrowski packs a knockout punch."

— *PUBLISHERS WEEKLY*, FOR *TKO*

"Refreshingly iconoclastic."

— *KIRKUS REVIEWS*, FOR *TKO*

"*TKO* is fast-paced, authentic, and funny as hell. Social worker and journeyman boxer Duffy Dombrowski is a workingman's hero, and I want him in my corner!"

— SEAN CHERCOVER, AUTHOR OF *TRINITY GAME*

"Not since Carl Hiassen's *Tourist Season* debut has there been a novel with such superb comic timing and laugh-out-loud lines."

— KEN BRUEN, SHAMUS AWARD-WINNING AUTHOR OF *THE GUARDS*, FOR *ON THE ROPES*

"An Everyman with a big heart and a wicked jab, Duffy Dombrowski may well be the new Spenser. I can't wait for Round Two."

— MARCUS SAKEY, AUTHOR OF *THE BLADE ITSELF*, FOR *ON THE ROPES*

"*On the Ropes* is sly, funny, irreverent, and one hell of a good time. Read it or be sorry you didn't. It's just that simple."

— LAURIEN BERENSON, AUTHOR OF *HOUNDED TO DEATH*

"It'll put you down for the count with laughter. Tom Schreck is a contender for funniest author working in the crime genre today."

— WILLIAM KENT KRUEGER, AUTHOR OF *THUNDER BAY*, FOR *ON THE ROPES*

# THE SPLIT DECISION

THE DUFFY DOMBROWSKI MYSTERIES

TOM SCHRECK

GLOVES OFF PUBLISHING

Library of Congress Control Number: 2025926818
Paperback ISBN: 978-1-971208-16-9
Digital Book ISBN: 978-1-971208-17-6

**1**

———————

It was quarter after eleven on a Tuesday morning in early March. Outside, the wind sliced through upstate New York like a dull knife, and inside, I was nursing a headache and had that edgy feeling you get from a shitty night of sleep.

Al, my basset hound, had dragged me outside three times last night—1:30, 3:00, and 5:00 a.m. Each time, he walked about eleven feet, stood there, and stared at me like I was the idiot in the situation. Then he barked to go back upstairs.

Don't ask me why.

I stood in my underwear, shivering, while he sat there, tail wagging. If dogs could laugh, Al had just told the best joke of his life.

We'd been together a decade, and I'd long since stopped trying to psychoanalyze him. He came into my life when a client of mine—one I thought I was helping—got herself murdered in county jail. I used to be a counselor at Jewish Unified Services, where I counseled addicts and the like.

Now, I owned a bar.

I wiped the bar down before closing last night, but I still

needed to restock the coolers. As I lifted longnecks from their cases, I could tell who'd been in recently. The Bud Light was low —Kelley. The Narragansett was nearly gone—Pasquale. And only two bottles of Schlitz left. That one was me.

Occupational hazard.

Duffy's at AJ's wasn't Studio 54. We had regulars, a few lunch-goers, but never a crowd. I didn't know what "industry standards" were supposed to be, but the bar had been left to me when AJ died, and I did what I could to keep it going.

SportsCenter murmured in the background. The baseball talking heads were arguing about why the Dodgers, who were supposed to be good, weren't going to be. Someone else was predicting a slump for the Yankees' home run king. It was another day at ESPN.

Then the front door opened.

The midmorning sun cut shadows across the floor, and for a second, I couldn't make out who it was. Eleven-thirty was early for my regulars.

Then he stepped forward.

The Caretaker.

His real name was Dush Pantamanjam, but nobody in Crawford called him that. He was an albino African American man with a wardrobe that made him look like he'd stepped out of a Bond film. Today, it was a black felt derby with an understated purple feather, a three-piece bespoke suit, and a gold pocket watch chain. Burgundy leather boots disappeared up his pant leg.

"Duffy, good to see you."

"Dush, what brings you in?" I said, using his real name just because I knew it chafed him a bit.

His lips twitched.

"I need your help."

That was new. Normally, I went to him. The Caretaker ran things in Crawford. He didn't sell drugs, but he knew who did. He wasn't a pimp, but they sought his blessing. He wasn't a loan shark, but the money flowed through him all the same. He made his cut through tributes sent up the line.

I poured myself a coffee. "Help with what?"

He adjusted his cuffs. "An associate of mine, who works with —ah—let's say, women of the night, came to me for assistance."

"A pimp?" I shook my head. "Dush, I may be intrepid and all that, but as you said, I've got to believe in the cause. Helping pimps isn't really my thing."

He nodded like he expected that. He let a beat pass before speaking again.

"Does the name Katherine Sullivan mean anything to you?"

The cold that ran through me had nothing to do with the wind outside.

"Kathy Sullivan was my high school girlfriend."

"I assume you lost touch, as young lovers often do."

"Yeah. It didn't end well." I frowned. "What does she have to do with this?"

"She was quite attractive, wasn't she?"

I felt the trap before I saw it. "Yeah, she was beautiful."

The Caretaker nodded. Let me sit with that for a second.

Then it hit me.

"You're not saying—"

"I'm afraid so." He smoothed the lapels of his coat. "She married, got bored, and found new pursuits. She became quite popular in the trade, so to speak. My associate and she formed a mutually beneficial business relationship."

I let that sink in.

"She commanded top dollar. Educated. Beautiful. Unlike most of the options available to her… clientele."

"You're telling me my old high school girlfriend is a—" I stopped myself.

"The politically sensitive term is now 'sex worker.'"

"Right." I rubbed my face. "And why are you telling me this?"

"She's missing."

I let that sink in, too.

"I want you to find her," he said.

I put down my coffee. "I don't think I'm your guy, Dush."

"My associate will pay you fifty thousand dollars."

That hung in the air between us. Fifty grand wasn't nothing. But this wasn't my thing. I'd stuck my nose in places it didn't belong a few times—probably against my better judgment—but I wasn't for hire.

Didn't like the feel of it.

"No thanks," I said.

The Caretaker didn't say anything for a long while. Just nodded. I didn't think he heard "no" too often, especially not when fifty grand was on the table.

Finally, he tipped his hat and half-smiled.

"So be it."

He rose from the barstool like a man who could make even that look elegant.

"Good day, Duffy."

And then he was gone.

2

K athy Sullivan.

A whore? A hooker? An escort? A sex worker?

I wasn't sure what to call it.

I'm the type that tends to spiral, and this one had some weight. The kind of thing that would have me staring at the ceiling instead of sleeping. Thinking. Overthinking. There was a sick feeling in my gut that I couldn't place.

Revolted? No.

Angry? Not really.

Embarrassed? Nah.

It felt like someone had stolen a piece of my adolescence. Kathy was my first girlfriend. My first love, if you can call it that at sixteen. What is it at sixteen? Love? Or just hormones, timing, and the simple thrill of being wanted?

Back then, it felt like everything. Intense. All-encompassing. Like I mattered in a way I hadn't before.

And then it ended. She went off to college. We swore distance wouldn't change anything. It didn't—until three weeks later, when the letter came.

There was another guy.

She swore there never would be.

I felt like the fool in every sad Top 40 song. Took me a long time to get right again.

That was a lifetime ago. Now, I knew better. People grow, change, become something else. I hadn't thought about her in years, but now that I was, I realized something—

I didn't know her at all.

Not now.

Maybe not then.

And now she was gone.

I wasn't sure what to make of that.

A couple of lunch crowd regulars came in—young office workers from the cookie factory down the street. They knew I could get them in and out in thirty minutes. A turkey club, a roast beef sandwich, and a ham and cheese pulled me out of my spiral, at least for a little while.

Then Jerry Number Two walked in.

Tie-dye shirt, jeans that had seen better days, and a Charles Bukowski book tucked under his arm. He slid onto his usual stool, and I put his Cosmo in front of him without asking.

He stared at me. I went back to staring at nothing.

Didn't take long.

"Duff, what's going on?"

"Nothin'," I said. "All good."

He kept looking at me. Nodded once. Didn't push.

I grabbed a bucket of ice and filled the already full sink.

Jerry didn't sip his drink. Didn't open his book. Just watched.

I sighed. "Got some news about an old girlfriend. Kind of messed me up."

"That TJ?" he asked. TJ was my on-again, off-again relationship. Mostly off. Probably permanently.

"No. First real girlfriend. From high school."

"Oh." He paused. "She sick? Dying?"

"No. Just found out what she's doing now."

Jerry took a slow sip of his drink. "Still gets you, huh? They always do."

"She's a hooker." The words fell out before I could dress them up.

Jerry blinked. "Makes rugs?"

I looked at him.

His face shifted, realization sinking in.

"Oh."

"Yeah. Oh."

"Geez, Duff." He swirled his drink. "That's gotta feel weird."

I shrugged. "High school was a long time ago." But even as I said it, I knew it wasn't that simple.

Agnes, my bloodhound and Al's unofficial sister, shuffled out from her alcove at the end of the bar. Liver and tan, wrinkles on top of wrinkles, she moved like she had all the time in the world. She put one heavy paw on Jerry's thigh.

Good timing. I needed the break.

Jerry scratched behind her ears. Agnes made a low, guttural sound of approval.

"When's the last time you saw her?" Jerry asked.

I thought about it. "First school break freshman year. I made the mistake of going to see her. Tried to plead my case. Lot of crying. Hurt like hell."

"First one always does."

"Yeah." I let out a breath. "Funny how you get hardened over the years. Doesn't mean breakups stop hurting, but at some point, you just expect them."

Kyrone came in. It was just after noon, so he was a bit early. Ky was a member, really the leader of the group made up of recovering addicts who met here most days around one. They were holdovers from my time at the clinic. They didn't like the woman who took over, so they came here to talk. None of them drank anything but coffee and soda while they were here.

"'Sup, D," Ky said by way of greeting. I was happy that I could drop the Jerry conversation.

"All good," I said. "Why are you here early?"

"Got nuthin' to do and didn't want to watch any more daytime TV."

"Fair enough," I said.

My phone chimed.

I pulled it from my pocket. "Duffy," came the voice on the other end. "Phillip Fowler here."

Fowler was my sort-of lawyer. The guy I called when something legal-ish needed doing. Lately, that meant dealing with the bar's creditors.

"The news isn't good," he said. His tone dropped. "The distributor isn't extending your credit. You can't order until you pay the past due. Sixteen grand."

I rubbed my temple. "What else?"

"The power and light. Four grand past due. Restaurant supply, six."

I exhaled through my nose. "If I give them something, you know, as a good faith payment, can I keep things running?"

Fowler hesitated. That wasn't like him.

"I think that time has passed," he said. "I'm sorry, Duffy, but you need to hear this. If you don't come up with the money, you don't have a choice. You're gonna have to shut down."

"Shut down?"

"You can't keep piling up debt."

I hadn't wanted to think about this. I'd been in denial. I thought this was just how businesses worked—always behind, always catching up.

I felt like a fool.

I signed off with Fowler, and I caught Ky looking me in the eye.

**3**

———————

Only three members of the recovery came in: Carl, the preppy middle-aged gay guy; and a newer young Latin woman named Sheena. Today, they were mostly self-run, talking about boredom and not being able to sleep. They performed the ritual of handing me a scratch-off lottery ticket. They gave me one from the whole group as payment for letting them meet here and drink free beverages. I threw themit under the register without looking at it.

Addicts didn't have a corner on that market.

By 7:30 that night, most of the usuals were in.

The *Foursome*—Rocco, Jerry Number One, TC, and Jerry Number Two—held their usual court. Rocco was in his sixties, built of hard fat and harder opinions. TC was a retired state worker whose thoughts mostly stirred confusion. Jerry Number One worked in heating and cooling, which neither raised nor lowered the group's collective IQ.

Jerry Number Two was back for a second session after taking a two-hour break, presumably to rest his liver.

Kelley, a city detective and my oldest friend, was nursing a

Bud Light. Pasquale, the bouncer from The Taco, the strip club down the street, had taken his usual stool. Built like a retired nose tackle, 'Squale was sharper than he looked—sharp enough to have won *Jeopardy!* once. It gave him a little rank in bar discussions.

But just a little.

"It's amazing," Rocco was saying, warming up to his favorite topic: obscure trivia. "Lincoln had a VP named Johnson. Kennedy had a VP named Johnson. Lincoln had a secretary named Kennedy, and Kennedy had a secretary named Lincoln."

"First or last?" TC asked.

Rocco frowned. "What?"

"First name or last name?"

"Last."

Rocco pushed ahead. "Booth ran from a theater, got caught in a warehouse. Oswald ran from a warehouse, got caught in a theater."

"Farmhouse," Jerry Number Two muttered.

"Oswald wasn't found in a farmhouse, you idiot," Rocco snapped.

"Booth."

"They found Oswald in a booth?" TC said. "I don't think that's right."

Rocco clenched his jaw and plowed forward. "And both Booth and Oswald have fifteen letters in their names."

"Is that counting Wilkes and Harvey?" TC asked.

"Who are they?" Jerry Number One said. "Did they work with the secretaries?"

It spiraled from there. Listening to them was like staring at one of those spinning hypnotic circles.

I turned my attention to Kelley. I opened a Bud Light and slid it to him.

"The assassinations. That's a new one," he said, half to himself.

"Be glad it's not *The Wizard of Oz* conspiracy, Rod Stewart, or Richard Gere."

Kelley smirked.

I debated whether I wanted to bring this up. Kelley wasn't exactly known for validating my thoughts and feelings.

I went for it anyway.

"You remember Kathy Sullivan?"

"Your high school heartthrob? How could I forget? You talked about her every night you got drunk. And back then, you got drunk every night."

"It wasn't that bad."

"If you say so." He took a sip of beer.

"You know what happened to her?"

"She went to Syracuse for college. Her folks moved. Never came back. I thought she got married. Something in finance, maybe?"

I nodded. "She was living back here. Not sure for how long."

Kelley gave me a look. "So, you finally stopped pining for TJ, you've got something semi-functional with Trina, and now you're romanticizing the one that got away when your face was still covered in zits?"

"Jesus, you have such a gentle way of putting things." I grabbed a Schlitz from the cooler.

"What's with the sudden fascination?"

I hesitated.

"I heard she's a... a... a—" I exhaled. "A hooker."

Kelley stopped mid-drink. Set his beer down. Studied me.

"Kathy?"

I nodded.

He turned that over in his head. Then something clicked. "Wait a minute. How'd you find that out?"

I got 'Squale a Narragansett to buy time.

Came back.

"Well?" Kelley said.

"The Caretaker told me."

Kelley pursed his lips. He hated The Caretaker. Hated that I had any relationship with him. He was, after all, a cop. And The Caretaker's business didn't exactly align with the goals of the police department.

"So, you and that freak are regular buds now? What, were you trying to score a kilo of product and this just came up?"

"He came here this morning. She's missing."

"And he just wanted you to know?"

I took a slow sip of Schlitz. Probably shouldn't have brought this up.

"He wants me to find her."

Kelley let that sit in the air. Then shook his head, disgusted.

"No. Don't tell me. I don't want to know."

He turned toward ESPN and took a long pull from his beer.

4

———

Kelley drained his beer and stood. "I gotta go."

He wasn't leaving because of our conversation. He was just Kelley—perpetually annoyed, except when he was winning. He slapped a twenty on the bar and walked out.

The *Foursome* was still locked in debate, and Kim and Pattie had settled in for the night. Kim had long dark hair, a smirk she wore like a trademark, and a devotion to Alabama football. White Claws were her drink of choice. Pattie was older, with salt-and-pepper hair, worked for the city, and had a memory like a steel trap. She drank Genesee drafts.

Pasquale was on his fourth or fifth Narragansett. Maybe sixth.

"I heard you and Kelley," he said, lifting the fresh beer to his lips. "Old high school flame's a sex worker, huh?"

"Yeah. Weird to process."

"You know what kind?"

I looked at him. I could tell he was dying to show off his knowledge.

"Not all sex work is the same, Duff." He swirled his beer.

"Big difference between someone working for drug money and a high-end escort with a business plan."

"Isn't there a joke about that? Something about agreeing on a price?"

"That's the punchline. But reality's messier." He leaned in. "Think about this: I work at *The Taco*. The girls get topless, do lap dances, touch, grind—would you call that prostitution?"

"No, that's stripping." I shrugged. "TJ did that."

"Okay. What if a guy—uh—gets a little *too* satisfied during the dance? Does that change anything?"

"Huh?"

"Gets a little… *release*." He raised an eyebrow.

I frowned. "You're losing me, 'Squal."

"That's my point. It's all relative. Some sex workers are victims—addicts with no choices, girls trafficked with no way out. But some? They're in it by choice. Some even see it as feminist power."

He drained the rest of his beer in one gulp.

"A feminist power position?" I asked.

"Think about it." He set his glass down. "The woman has what the guy wants. He's paying *her*. She's in control. He's the pawn."

I let that roll around in my head. On an intellectual level, maybe. On a real-world level? Thinking about body parts, transactions, and the smell of sweat—it didn't seem all that powerful to me.

"What about the women at *The Taco*?" I asked.

"What about them?"

"Are they hooking on the side?"

"They're not supposed to. But most aren't local. They

bounce up and down the coast. Wouldn't be surprised if some have sites."

"Sites?"

"Everything's online now. It's safer, more anonymous. The smart ones go independent."

"So, pimps are out of business?"

'Squal shook his head. "Nah. They just control the websites instead of the street corners." He took another long sip. "Maybe your old flame figured it out. Maybe she's running her own show."

I chewed on that.

"So, what? You're telling me this isn't some tragic sob story? That Kathy picked this career, owns it, and maybe even sees it as *empowering?*"

My sarcasm was thick. Maybe a little bitter.

'Squal shrugged. "Why not?

**5**

———————

After the bar cleared out, I took Al and Agnes for a walk. Crawford at night was like most mid-sized cities during the week—quiet, slowed down. The soundscape changed. A car in the distance. A bus rattling by. A random drunk yelling at a lamppost. It reminded you that you weren't alone, even if your company at this hour wasn't the kind you'd keep in daylight.

Agnes was in a sniffy mood, stopping at every bush and patch of dirt like she was conducting a full-scale investigation. Al, meanwhile, walked in a straight line, determined. The contrast kept my arms stretched uncomfortably wide.

A microcosm of how I felt.

"Yo, Duffy!" The familiar voice knocked me out of my reverie. It was Lorenzo, from the gym. "What are you doing out at this hour?" 'Zo was my assistant at the gym, a top heavyweight contender and a guy who came with some history.

"I am at the mercy of my bosses." I motioned to the dogs. "How 'bout you?"

"Ah, on my way home. I check on some girls I know. Headin' home," he said.

"See you at the gym," I said, and we parted to go our own ways.

I went back to thinking. Maybe not my best activity.

My bar—the business I never asked for—was failing. *Duffy's at AJ's* had meaning, but mostly because of what it had been before it belonged to me. If I bailed, it would be gone. The memories, the camaraderie, the ridiculous debates over Kennedy/Lincoln coincidences.

Or would they?

Memories don't need real estate. The *Foursome* would find another clubhouse. I'd still drink somewhere. Things wouldn't be the same, but they'd go on.

And then there was Kathy.

My high school love. Now a sex worker. Or, as 'Squal put it, a *feminist in a power position.*

I wasn't exactly buying that. It was hard to see empowerment in something that involved bodily fluids and strangers with cash. But I wasn't enlightened. Never claimed to be.

What mattered was that she was missing.

Technically, not a case for law enforcement. No signs of foul play. No one had reported her missing. She was an adult. But The Caretaker said she needed help, and for all his connections to the underworld, the man's word was solid.

And then there was the money.

Fifty grand would save the bar. Hell, it would give me breathing room. Sure, it wouldn't fix everything. I'd still have no direction, no meaningful relationship, and no real plan for my future. But solvency was a good start.

And if I was being honest with myself, there was something else.

I liked this kind of thing. The unknown. The danger. It made me feel alive. More alive than stocking coolers and playing audience to *The Wizard of Oz* conspiracies.

By the time we reached the apartment, my mind was made up.

The bar was part of the same building, just upstairs. Maybe that was the problem—my whole life was contained within these four walls. Maybe that's why I felt stale.

There was something else, too. I wasn't fighting much anymore. I ran the Y's boxing program after Smitty bailed, but that cut into my own time in the ring. I was getting older. The window for a professional fight was closing.

Not sure how I got here. I was in charge of two things I cared about but never chose.

I could've refused both. But I didn't.

Maybe because I never chose anything else. So I let them choose me.

That didn't feel great.

Back inside, Al and Agnes got fed. Agnes curled up on the couch, spinning three times before collapsing like a demolished skyscraper. Al claimed my bed, in my spot, and started snoring immediately.

I poured a couple of fingers of Jim Beam and added one ice cube. I slid my hands under Al and dragged him across the comforter. I'd gotten so good at it that he didn't even pause his snore.

I propped up some pillows, took a sip, and flipped on *Law & Order*.

Adam Schiff was pissed off at Jack McCoy about something.

The old man never liked taking risks and didn't like the idea of losing in court.

"Make the deal!" he barked.

He didn't want to gamble if he didn't have to.

I think I knew how he felt.

**6**

———

I went to The Caretaker's storefront in Jefferson Hill.

*The Hill* was Crawford's version of a rundown shopping district—six blocks of bargain sneakers, knockoff watches, and Yankees hats in colors the team had never worn. Every brim had that big silver sticker, and the guys who bought them never took it off.

At the back of the store, a twenty-something kid manned the counter. He wore a Pittsburgh Grays jersey and a matching cap, slouched like gravity had given up on him.

"Caretaker in?" I asked.

He gave me the slow, unimpressed once-over.

"Who you?" he said, efficiently cutting the sentence down by removing the verb.

"Duffy. He knows me."

The kid disappeared behind a curtain, moving just enough to remain technically alive. A low murmur of conversation, then he came back and gave me a nod.

I stepped through.

The Caretaker sat behind his ornate Victorian desk, the brass banker's lamp casting a warm glow over a leather-bound journal. A Mont Blanc fountain pen rested in his hand, which he carefully set aside as I entered.

He wore a Glen plaid vest with chains looping between the pockets. The matching suit coat hung neatly behind him on a wooden three-legged coat rack.

"Mr. D, I am surprised to see you."

"I'll take the job," I said. This place always made me feel out of place, like I had accidentally stepped into the wrong century.

"Splendid." He steepled his fingers. "I'm curious about the change of heart, but I won't pry."

"Tell me more about the situation. Do you have a photo of Kathy?"

He opened a drawer and slid a manila envelope across the desk.

I pulled out an 8x10 glossy. A platinum blonde in a low-cut evening gown, a high slit revealing a shapely thigh. The makeup was flawless—glamorous but not overdone. The photo was professional, the kind you'd see in a high-end escort ad.

Then I flipped through the others.

They weren't for advertising.

The first: she was naked, bent over, gripping her ankles above patent leather stilettos.

The second: a close-up, eyes closed, lips wrapped around a well-endowed man.

The third: her and another woman, tangled in each other.

My throat went dry..

I forced myself to stay neutral, but it wasn't easy. The platinum hair, the surgically enhanced body, the sculpted cheekbones—none of it matched the girl I knew. But it was her.

And now I was a voyeur.

I set the photos down and exhaled slowly.

The Caretaker watched me. His expression was unreadable, but I could tell he was gauging my reaction.

"She goes by Kathy now?" My voice felt rougher than usual.

"Yes. She's still listed on the website."

He handed me a printout of the homepage.

*"Platinum Experience."*

A collage of beautiful women in expensive but revealing evening wear. No menus, no links, just a login screen. No way to join. No way to contact.

"Questions?" the Caretaker asked.

"Yeah, a bunch." I forced myself to focus. "Do we know her location? Any clientele? What exactly does this business do?"

"I believe it does precisely what we imagine it does."

"Which is?"

He smiled. "A high-end escort service, Mr. Duffy. But not just any escort service. One designed to cater to those of exceptional means and particular tastes."

"Do we know where she is?"

"No. My associate has tried to reach her. She is not responding. Calls, texts—nothing."

"Who's the associate?"

He slid a business card across the desk.

*Joe Carlton*

*A phone number.*

That was it.

"Carlton? The guy who wants her found?"

"Yes, yes he is."

I pocketed the card. "Great."

I stood, tucking the photos and the website printout back into the envelope.

The Caretaker watched me, his lips curling slightly.

"Good luck, Mr. Duffy."

It sounded less like well-wishes and more like a warning.

**7**

----

I had explicit photos of my high school girlfriend seared into my brain. I needed some mental floss.

And I needed fifty grand.

*Platinum Experience.* The name itself dripped with pretension. It wasn't just an escort service—it was a *luxury experience.* A way for rich men to convince themselves they weren't desperate losers paying for sex. No, they were *connoisseurs of pleasure.*

The thing was, I didn't know how any of this actually worked.

Sure, I'd heard of escort services. There were websites, ads, vague euphemisms. But what was the *real* process? Did you place an order like a pizza? Was there a secret code word, some coy dance of innuendo?

I wasn't a prude, and in the abstract, the idea was... intriguing. No-strings sex with beautiful women who'd do whatever you wanted. That was every guy's fantasy, right?

But the fantasy and the reality weren't the same thing. The fantasy was a Bond movie. The reality involved body fluids and cash transactions.

I pulled up *Platinum Experience* on my phone.

The website dripped wealth. *Luxury experiences.Attention to your every need.More than your imagination will allow.*

My imagination could allow for a lot.

I dialed the number.

"You have reached Platinum Experience. At the beep, please enter your passcode."

I punched in six random numbers.

"That is not a valid code."

So much for that.

How did anyone even get in? There wasn't exactly a *Prostitution for Dummies* guide. No *Consumer Reports: The Escort Edition.*

I glanced at the stack of *Crawland* tabloids we kept at the bar. They were free, full of ads for questionable massage parlors, escort services, and live cam performers.

The back pages were a crash course in coded sex work.

- "A-Level" meant anal.
- "BBS" meant unprotected sex.
- "BS" meant body slide, which probably had nothing to do with water parks.
- "GFE" meant *Girlfriend Experience*.

I wondered if that meant she'd tell you to pick a restaurant, then veto all your choices.

By the time I finished decoding the escort alphabet, I was less intrigued and more bored.

Still, this was *Kathy's* world now. If I wanted to find her, I needed to understand it.

I called Reno. Reno was a guy I'd known for my whole life.

We went to high school together. He wasn't a criminal but operated on the margins of the street. Reno knew shit.

He strolled into the bar at 1:45, wearing a faded Yankees t-shirt and jeans with a genuine, non-fashionable rip in the knee.

I slid a 7&7 in front of him.

"Flattered you remembered," he said. "So what's up?"

I leaned in. "What do you know about the escort situation in Crawford?"

Reno raised an eyebrow. "Hookers? What are you, Sinatra? Gonna round up the Rat Pack?"

"You know what I mean. How does *Platinum Experience* work?"

He sipped his drink. "You mean, how do you find them? How much it costs? How to pass the STD test?"

"I'm looking for someone who's gone missing."

"Aren't we all..." Reno muttered. Then he held out his hand. "What do you got?"

I slid him the envelope from The Caretaker.

He flipped through the photos. His eyebrows shot up. "Damn. This is *Platinum Experience*, alright. Top shelf. They're owned by some big outfit in Manhattan."

He kept staring at the pictures longer than necessary.

"Any idea how to get in?" I asked.

"They don't just let anybody in. Usually, you need a referral. A way to weed out the creeps who just want to call and send, uh... pics."

I frowned. "Pics?"

"You know." He gestured toward his lap.

Jesus.

"I try not to judge," Reno said, sipping his drink.

"If you were trying to find someone, how would you do it?"

"I'd get a referral. Someone who's in the system. Then, you get a password, log in, and check the roster." He shrugged. "Or you could just show these photos to someone who might recognize her."

I nodded. "She's not responding to her… uh, *associate*."

Reno smirked. "You mean her *pimp*?"

"I hear he's not a pimp. More of a… intermediary."

Reno looked at me like I had two heads.

"A rose by any other name…" he muttered.

I realized how stupid I sounded.

"Is there any danger in this?" I asked.

"You mean besides getting arrested or needing to see a priest after?"

I shook my head. "I mean, is *she* in danger?"

Reno set down his glass. "Look, the street girls you saw at the clinic? They're twenty bucks a pop, turning it over to a pimp for a hit of crack. *Platinum Experience* is another world. The girls there are educated, classy. Hell, they probably know how to order off a wine list." He tapped the photo. "This one? She's making real money. Two grand minimum, probably a lot more."

"So it's not trafficking?"

Reno leaned back. "If you're asking if she's chained in a basement somewhere? No. But she's still got a boss. She can't just walk away."

He picked up Kathy's headshot again.

His eyes narrowed.

"Wait a minute." He tapped the photo. "I *know* her. Kathy… Kathy Sullivan?"

I exhaled slowly. "Yeah."

Reno let out a low whistle. "Damn, Duff. She didn't look like this back in high school."

He flipped through the rest of the photos. I snatched them back and slid them into the envelope.

"She doesn't need saving," Reno said. "If she's in *Platinum*, she's making bank." He smirked. "Hell, she's doing better than us."

"She's still a whore, isn't she?" I said.

Reno glanced around the bar, then back at me.

"You do this bar gig for money, right?"

"Yeah."

"You love every second of it? The puke mopping, the drunk idiots?"

I sighed. "It comes with the job."

"Well," Reno said, taking another sip, "Kathy's just got a different job description."

I stared at him. The moral relativism was giving me whiplash.

I needed to focus.

"Where do I start?" I asked.

Reno scratched his chin. "I know a guy with a password. I'll see if he'll hook you up."

I nodded. "Couldn't hurt."

And just like that, I had a way in.

8

_______

That night, the bar was packed, at least by my standards.

The *Foursome* were in. So were Kelley, Pasquale, Kim, and Pattie. A couple of new regulars occupied their usual booth, and three guys from the cookie factory were finishing their shift drinks.

Kelley was quieter than usual, his mood hovering between pissy and brooding, which meant I left him alone.

"Well, they went and found another one," Rocco said.

With a *flourish*, he folded his *New York Post* and creased it with unnecessary precision, as if the world desperately needed this edition preserved.

Nobody took the bait.

We were all waiting on Final Jeopardy.

The answer: "This Irish-American was the first champion in pugilism after the institution of the Marquis de Queensberry rules..."

"Teddy Roosevelt!" TC shouted.

"That ain't it," Jerry Number Two said.

"I think the Marquis is the key here…" Jerry mused. "What do we know about Marquises?"

"Big car," Rocco offered.

'Squal nodded toward me. "Duffy knows this one."

I sighed. I did.

"Sullivan. John L."

"Wrong!" 'Squal said.

I frowned.

"Oh, shit—*Who was* John L. Sullivan?"

'Squal, being a former *Jeopardy!* champ, was a stickler for format.

"Duff, man, c'mon. Proper rules."

I shook my head.

Rocco waved his *Post* again. "Okay, but can we talk about the alligator they found in the New York sewers?"

TC groaned. "Urban legend."

Jerry Number Two nodded. "That's not real, Rocco."

"Eight million people in New York and *not one* of them flushed a gator?"

Before anyone could argue, the TV cut in with a breaking news teaser.

"Three sex workers murdered in Crawford. Full story at eleven."

Silence.

Kelley stood, drained his beer, and walked straight to the door. Didn't say a word. I knew that meant he'd be working late.

Trina, who had just walked in, stared at the screen, then at me.

"Oh my God," she said. "I hope they aren't from the clinic."

A fair number of women who cycled through the clinic

worked the streets to feed their habits. Some had pimps. Some didn't. Either way, they were at the bottom of the ladder.

"Did you know any of them?" I asked.

"Not well," she said. "Some would make small talk while waiting for their session."

"How bad was it?"

She hesitated. "The sex work? They never talked about it directly, but you could tell. They were rough. Missing teeth. Cheap extensions. It was just… part of the cycle. I don't think they even thought about it. That would take years of clean time and therapy."

I nodded. Thought of Kathy.

"Do you ever get *higher-end* sex workers at the clinic?"

Trina gave me a look. "Higher-end? Like *Pretty* Woman?" She rolled her eyes. "Duff, *you remember the clinic, don't* you?"

"Yeah," I admitted.

I exhaled. Took a sip of Schlitz.

"Hey, can I talk to you upstairs?"

She raised an eyebrow but nodded. When we went upstairs, it usually meant something serious.

'Squal slid behind the bar. The *Foursome* had already left, leaving only Kim and Pattie. The dogs stayed behind as Trina and I headed up.

I poured her more wine and grabbed a Schlitz. Then, I pulled out the envelope.

"I need your opinion on something."

She took the headshot first.

"Very attractive…" she said. Then, she flipped to the others.

She paused.

"Oh."

"Yeah."

Trina set the photos down.

"What are you looking for from me?"

I exhaled. "I guess I just… I don't know. I'm trying to figure out *who* she is now. *What's going on with* her."

She picked up the second picture—the one of Kathy servicing a guy. She held it up.

"This?" She tapped the photo. "This is what's going on with her."

"Is it possible she's *okay* with it?" I asked.

Trina's sarcasm was thick enough to spread on toast.

"You mean *the feminist* stance?" she said. "The idea that sex work is empowering, that women hold the power because *men pay* them?"

"…Yeah."

She didn't say anything. She just held up the photo again.

"Does this look like a woman in power to you?"

I didn't answer right away.

"Couldn't it just be *work*? Something she's fine with?"

Trina exhaled. "I find it very hard to believe that someone can detach themselves from being penetrated for money, dealing with *secretions*, and then just *shrug it off* at the end of the day."

"So she's *damaged*?" I said.

Trina sipped her wine. "Duff, consent means *choosing to do something of your own free will*, right?"

"Yeah."

"Well, by that standard, the girls at the clinic are 'choosing' to walk the street for twenty bucks."

I didn't answer.

She swirled her glass. "Possible she's *fully aware* and *fine* with it? Sure. But *likely*?" She shook her head.

I ran a hand over my face.

"And someone just murdered three of her peers," she said.

"Yeah," I muttered. "There's that."

She studied me for a moment. "Duff, what the hell are you doing? Are you trying to *save* her?"

"No."

Trina let the silence stretch before she spoke again.

"…Then what?"

I sighed.

"The money."

She frowned. "Since when have you been driven by money?"

I took a sip of Schlitz.

"I'm gonna lose the bar," I said.

I didn't look at her when I said it.

**9**

———————

The *Union Times* headlined the murders the next morning.

THREE SEX WORKERS EXECUTED IN CRAWFORD.
CONNECTIONS UNCLEAR.

If it bleeds, it leads.
The victims were from different corners of the industry.

- Juanita Morris was a webcam model and street prostitute. She performed live on *Spankview.com*, a cam site with thousands of daily users. Shot once in the head. No forced entry. Likely knew her killer.
- Terrie Bosco starred in low-budget amateur porn, her videos uploaded to *Pornstop*, a streaming site with 220,000 paying subscribers. Same execution-style murder.
- Lana McShay was an escort. The article noted she worked for Platinum Experience, listing her overnight rate at $1,200. No explicit mention of illegal activity,

but the paper didn't dance around the implications.

Same gunshot to the head.


Three different women. Three different versions of sex work. Same method of execution.

I set the paper down.

This wasn't random.

I grabbed my laptop and started digging.

*Spankview.com* was part of a network of webcam models—thousands of women broadcasting live for paying subscribers. Clicking deeper, I found that *Spankview* was owned by Mindfun.

Never heard of it.

I checked *Pornstop*. The "About" page confirmed it. Also owned by Mindfun.

Back to *Platinum Experience*. No visible ownership info. No *Mindfun* branding. But now I was curious.

A quick Wikipedia search hit me with this:

Mindfun is a multinational adult entertainment conglomerate owned by a private equity firm. It operates escort services, streaming platforms, and adult content production with an estimated multi-billion-dollar annual revenue. Its corporate headquarters are in Luxembourg, shielding it from U.S. regulations and tax laws.

Billions.

This wasn't a street-level operation. This was corporate sex work.

I needed more information.

I called Rick.

Rick and I used to box together. He went to night school, got into finance, and now spent his days playing the stock market instead of trading punches.

It was barely 7 AM, but he was already at his desk.

"I ain't got much time, Duff, market's about to open."

"You know anything about Mindfun?"

"The porn conglomerate? Yeah, they're huge. Private firm, worth billions."

"From making dirty movies?"

Rick laughed. "Porn accounts for 35% of all downloads on the internet. 40 million people watch daily. That's a whole lot of *dirty movies.*"

"Who runs it? Some greasy guy with a mustache?"

"More like a Harvard MBA."

I paused. "You're kidding."

"They might as well be making toasters. Corporate offices, cubicles, board meetings. Except one floor, where only select employees have access."

"Jesus."

"It's all about supply and demand, Duff. And trust me, the demand is *huge.*" He chuckled. "Hey, gotta strategize. Market's opening."

Click.

I poured coffee. Fed the dogs.

*What the hell did I get myself into?*

Billions of dollars.

Ivy League executives.

Corporate porn, corporate escorts, corporate sex.

This wasn't some seedy underground operation. It was as structured as Amazon—except instead of shipping packages, they were selling people.

I thought back to when I was a kid.

If you wanted porn, you stole a Playboy off the top rack at the gas station. Maybe if you were really adventurous, you grabbed a Penthouse, wrapped in plastic with a censored paper sleeve hiding the cover.

If you were lucky, you found a dirty magazine in the woods, next to empty beer cans and cigarette butts. That was the world of sex work back then—hidden, shameful, something men whispered about.

Now?

Now, it was a billion-dollar industry on your $700 smartphone.

And it wasn't just *nudes* anymore. It was streaming, interactive, custom-made experiences.

I had my own theory on it.

Porn was like drugs. Start small, and after a while, you need something stronger to get the same rush. If you showed a fourteen-year-old porn user a 1980s Playboy, he'd probably laugh at it.

I wondered what this meant for real relationships. For how men and women connected.

Maybe some shame and guilt weren't the worst thing in the world.

Maybe I was just old-fashioned.

Or maybe I was okay with that.

**10**

———

I stopped off at the gym to watch the afternoon youth program.

The Crawford YMCA wasn't one of those fancy, suburban Y's that catered to yoga moms and finance bros. No shiny new weight racks or wellness centers. It was brick and sweat and history.

The place smelled like chlorine, pine disinfectant, and bodies that had worked too hard for too long. The basketball court was so layered in faded paint from decades of different sports that it was hard to tell where one game ended and another began.

Fat Eddie worked the locker room.

Seventies. Gay. Snarky as hell. Had been handing out towels to naked athletes for thirty years. He had long ago landed his dream job.

"What's up, Eddie?" I said as I passed his cage.

"Just soaking it all in," he said, deadpan.

He'd been using that same line for as long as I'd known him.

I headed downstairs to the boxing gym. The sounds were familiar.

The rhythmic rat-a-tat-tat of the speed bag.

The sharp exhales of punches landing on pads.

The calls of a trainer, yelling out combinations.

Lorenzo ran today's session. Trevon, our top amateur fighter, helped out. Fifteen years old. 15-2 record. Reigning Silver Gloves champ. Smart kid. B average. Lives in a supervised apartment. Lorenzo had taken him under his wing, the way Smitty once took me.

The class had eight or ten kids, depending on the day. Today, they were lined up as Lorenzo called out punches. Trevon walked the line, correcting stances, adjusting footwork.

*Repetition.*

It was the same way Smitty taught me.

Boxing was like playing the guitar. If your fundamentals were garbage, all the aggression in the world didn't mean shit.

Today, Lorenzo and Trevon were like father and son, maybe closer. They both made each other grow. Lorenzo had something to live for besides ghetto values. He told me his mother was a street hooker and took a lot of abuse, some right in front of him.

Trevon's mom was an addict whose whereabouts were unknown. His father was a local dealer and an all-around piece of shit. He was abusive to Tre and the reason he lived in a home.

You could see the pride in Tre because Zo cared for him. It gave him worth. It gave him cred. It made him something.

Smitty ran the gym. He was my trainer, my corner man, and the closest thing I had to a mentor. Then one day, his brother died, leaving behind a special needs son. Smitty was gone in two days.

And the gym fell apart.

A bad element crept in, bringing drugs, thugs, and disrespect. The worst of it?

That bad element was led by Lorenzo, who at the time was a big-time prospect on track to be the heavyweight champion of the world. He was ghetto, with ghetto hangers-on who disrespected the gym, took advantage of some kids, blasted music with bad language, and before long the place was a mess. Lorenzo and I had a "Come-to-Jesus" moment in the ring, and though he was younger, faster, and more naturally skilled than me, I gave him a beating in front of his posse.

How was I able to beat up a younger, stronger, more athletically gifted fighter?

I cheated.

My years in gyms, small dirty fight cards, and other gyms gave me a schooling. Boxing has a long learning curve, and even though it is sanctioned and organized violence, there are things that you can learn that are outside the lines. In this case, a well-placed elbow and a forehead-slamming headbutt loosened the younger fighter up.

After that, I lost my shit. It is what Kelley calls "Going Duffy." I smashed the fancy Bluetooth speaker in front of the ghetto posse and ordered them all out of my gym. That was the day I became in charge.

Smitty taught me the dirty tricks. He cautioned that they were illegal and probably immoral but that I should know them in case I ever had cause to use them. The gym was cause.

A few months later, Lorenzo came back to the gym and asked me if I would train him. I'm still not sure why, but I've watched him blossom into a man. He's still a competitive fighter, though a couple of losses have kept him off the fast track to a title shot. He connected with Trevon, who was living in a group home without much support until Lorenzo showed an interest in him.

I hear from Smitty once in a while. He's not much of a talker, and he's getting older. He has his hands full with his nephew, and when I talk to him, I can hear the fatigue in his voice. I've learned life has a way of doing that.

Smitty never really sat me down for any lectures on life. He harped on fundamentals and putting in the work, and the power of showing up and doing the same things over and over to get better. He wanted me to be honorable and decent in and out of the gym because that's just how things should be. One time I had a fight in Tennessee with this country boy who had a 14-0 record and was making some regional noise. I was brought in, like I often was, as an opponent and to lose.

At weigh-in, he spouted racist bullshit, directing most of it at Smitty.

I fought my ass off that night, but it didn't matter. I was losing. That prick was about to have his hand raised.

I couldn't let that happen.

I positioned myself so the rookie ref couldn't see. I threw a right hook, deliberately short, so my elbow caught his temple. He staggered, and I pounced. By the time the ref pulled me off, he had two broken orbitals, a concussion, and a fractured jaw. He never fought again.

The crowd threw beer bottles at us. We left town in the middle of the night.

Once we made it to a motel off the highway, I waited for Smitty to lecture me.

Tell me I had crossed a line. Tell me I did the wrong thing. Instead, he cracked open a beer and took a sip.

"Nice job, kid," he said.

I'm still not sure what I learned that night. Maybe it was that sometimes rules need to be broken. That sometimes the ends justify the means. That there's a moment when you stop playing by the book and take control.

Watching the kids in the gym, I thought about what lay ahead.

And I realized—

I was going to have to apply what Smitty taught me.

**11**

---

The next morning, I called Joe Carlton.

He picked up on the second ring and answered like a cop.

"Carlton."

"This is Duffy. The Caretaker—" He didn't let me finish.

"Oh yeah. The fighter. You're gonna find Kathy."

"Well, I'm gonna try."

"You eat yet?"

"No, but I—"

"Meet me at the Blue Ribbon Diner in half an hour."

Click.

Well, Joe really liked to get to the point.

The Blue Ribbon Diner was one of those always-crowded joints with a 3,000-item menu and a cheesecake that people would actually fight over. I had nothing else to do, so I headed out early.

On the way, I tried to picture what Carlton might look like.

A velour track suit? Gold medallion over a hairy chest? Or

the Tony Soprano look? Big arms, soft belly over hard fat, balding but too rich to care?

Turned out, I was way off.

"You Duffy?"

The guy standing next to me at the counter was lean, fit, and dressed like a country club retiree. Salmon-colored Ralph Lauren polo. Crisp pleated khakis. Tasseled loafers. Late fifties, maybe. Long hair, Mediterranean features.

We shook hands.

"Let's get a booth," he said.

On the way, he greeted every waitress by name. When we slid into a circular booth in the back, I got the sense that this was his booth.

"Dush tell you much about me?" he asked.

"Didn't tell me anything."

Carlton smirked.

"That's Dush. He didn't get where he is by blabbering."

I waited. He'd get to it eventually.

The waitress came by.

"Mo, the usual. Duff, whatyawant? On me."

"I'm good."

I was hungry. For some reason, I just didn't feel like eating.

Mo slid Carlton's breakfast in front of him—scrambled eggs, sausage, pancakes, orange juice.

"Sure you don't want something?"

I waved him off.

Carlton cut to it.

"Kathy is special. She started with Sugar Daddy stuff," he said.

I frowned. "What's that?"

Carlton dabbed orange juice from his chin. "It's like… casual escorting. No price list. No formal agreement. Just an unspoken deal—older guys take care of you, you take care of them."

"How common is that?"

"More than you think. College girls, maybe some women a little older. It's a fine line between dating and pay-for-play."

He cut into his sausage. "Kathy wasn't in college, though. She was divorced, restless, and broke. She went home with a guy one night. He gave her a 'gift' afterward. Next time, she joked about money, and it became a habit."

He chewed. Swallowed. "The guy was a country club type, twenty-five years older. Liked bragging to his golf buddies about her."

I didn't say anything.

"She leaned into it. Instead of getting embarrassed, she asked, playfully, if his friends wanted a turn."

I blinked.

"Before you know it, she's got six Sugar Daddies, a new car, and a paid-for condo."

"So… that's when she became a pro?"

He shook his head.

"Not really. There was no price list. Just 'dates' and 'gifts.'"

I leaned back. "And this is normal?"

"Oh yeah. Makes rich guys feel cool, not desperate."

He speared some eggs.

"A while after that, she found me," Carlton said. "She wanted to know what being a real pro was like and what she could make. She had a head for finance."

"Why'd she need you?"

"Safety. Clients. She didn't want to deal with low-rent guys. That's my job."

I stared at him.

"So… you're a pimp."

His eyes darkened.

"Do I look like a pimp?" he said. "You think I got a purple Stetson and a fur coat in the back of my El Dorado?"

I shrugged.

"I run logistics. I find safe, high-end clients. She pays me a percentage. It's business. Eventually I referred her to Platinum."

I watched him pick up a strip of bacon and take a bite.

"Who owns Platinum Experience?"

"Not me. I referred her there."

"Then who?"

He hesitated. "Hard to say."

"Mob stuff?"

Carlton sighed. "Kid, this isn't TV. It's corporate, not street-level. She's a high-value asset."

I let that settle.

"You up for finding her?" Carlton asked. "Dush tell you what it's worth?"

"Yeah." I looked at my cold, oversweetened coffee. "Seems like a lot of money to find a…"

I trailed off.

Carlton smirked. "Gives you an idea of what kind of earner she is."

I exhaled. "You got any leads?"

Carlton twirled his fork in the air.

"Try booking a date with her

I stared at him. "A date."

"She's not answering me. But if she's still working, you might be able to buy your way in."

I left the diner with a full stomach of nothing and a bad taste in my mouth.

I was going to have to book an appointment with my high school girlfriend.

## 12

That night at the bar, I had trouble concentrating.

Part of it was Kathy. The rest of it was trying to untangle the world she had gotten into.

I wasn't naïve. People paid for sex. Always have. Always will. But when I actually looked at how it worked—the mechanics of it—it got murkier.

There were men who bought sex like a subscription service. Sugar Daddies who paid for the illusion of a relationship—someone who wouldn't fight over where to eat, who wouldn't nag, who wouldn't leave their hair clogging the drain.

I mean, it was efficient. No broken hearts. No baggage. Just pay a fee and get what you want.

But it felt so goddamn empty.

I was still stuck on that when Pasquale waved a hand in front of my face.

"Earth to Duff… Earth to Duff…"

I blinked.

"Oh. Yeah. What do you need?"

Pasquale raised an eyebrow. "Really?"

I sighed and grabbed him a Narragansett. Seven left in the cooler. The distributor wouldn't front me more.

I got a sick feeling in my gut.

I slid the beer across the bar. Pasquale took half of it in a single gulp.

"How's the search going?" Pasquale asked.

"Weird," I said. "Met a guy who brokered Kathy's deal into Platinum Experience. He's the one who wants her found. He made it real clear—this is an organized crime thing."

Pasquale nodded. "No big surprise."

"No, I guess not. But why were three women killed? And why all from businesses connected to Mindfun?"

Pasquale wiped some foam from his lip.

"Hard to picture that as a coincidence."

I grabbed him another Narragansett. Six left.

"Duff, I think you gotta go see an escort somehow. Book a session. Ask questions."

I exhaled through my nose.

"One problem—I don't have a grand to blow on an appointment." I hesitated. "Two—how do I even do that? Ask questions during foreplay? 'Hey, sweetheart, before we get started, can you tell me if you've seen my missing ex-girlfriend?'"

Pasquale smirked. "Probably not the best icebreaker."

"And three," I added, "I'm not keen on poking around in a mob-run business."

Pasquale downed the rest of his beer. I got him another. Five.

"I can set you up with one of the girls at The Taco. They travel in that world, even if they're not exactly in it."

I turned that over in my head.

"That might help."

The two Jerrys walked in at the same time. They didn't ride together, but sometimes, they arrived in sync—like some kind of cosmic alignment. I got their drinks and checked in on Pattie and Kim. Pattie was telling Kim about someone she knew in high school 45 years ago.

Then Kelley walked in and he looked drained.

I slid him a Bud Light. Maybe a case left in the fridge.

"How's work?" I asked.

Kelley took a sip and let out a slow breath. "The murder investigation has the whole department jacked up."

"How so?"

"There's no evidence of anything." He set the bottle down. "Clean. Too clean."

I frowned. "Like, professional?"

Kelley nodded.

I glanced at Pasquale.

"But why?" I asked.

Kelley rubbed the back of his neck. "That's the thing. No one knows."

He took another sip, then added:

"The girls—excuse me, sex workers—weren't street-level. They weren't strung out. No signs of a stalker. No serial killer pattern." He hesitated. "Single gunshot to the head. No sexual activity before death."

I didn't ask how they knew that. I didn't really want to.

"So what's left?" I asked.

Kelley shrugged.

Pasquale swirled his beer and said:

"A message."

I turned to him.

"Someone is sending a message."

## 13

"What kind of message?" I asked.

Kelley gave Pasquale a look—the kind that said *let the real cops do the thinking.*

Pasquale wasn't fazed. He took a sip of beer, swirled it in the glass, then looked at the ceiling like he was picking a theory from the air.

"Could be a religious nut—thinks he's cleansing the world of sin," he said. "Could be a disgruntled customer who got ripped off. Could be a random serial killer." He shrugged. "Or it could be business."

"Business?" I asked.

Pasquale set down his glass. "When rival gangs sell drugs, what do they do?"

"They kill each other," I said.

"Right. So, why wouldn't the sex business be the same?"

I turned to Kelley. He didn't look convinced.

"Carlton said Platinum was connected," I reminded him.

"Yeah, but when a business gets this corporate, do they still solve problems with bullets?" I asked. "They've got money.

Lawyers. Bank accounts. They don't need to go old-school, do they?"

Pasquale leaned in. "That depends on the stakes."

Kelley sighed. "Here we go…"

"No, seriously," Pasquale said. "If some outside entity was threatening Platinum, what's their play? They can't go to the cops. They can't file a complaint with the Better Business Bureau. If the money's big enough, people start getting removed."

Kelley didn't argue.

I rubbed my jaw. "So, what? Some other outfit is trying to muscle in?"

Pasquale shrugged. "Would Carlton know if they were?"

"He should," I said. "He didn't mention anything about it."

Pasquale smirked. "Then maybe **he's lying.**"

Kelley sighed, then checked his watch.

"I can't believe I'm listening to this shit." He grabbed his beer. "You two—"

Then his phone rang. The second he answered it, his whole body changed. His posture stiffened. His voice dropped.

"Kelley." A pause. "When?"

I sat up.

"Where?"

He listened. His jaw clenched.

"Name?"

I felt something cold settle in my gut.

"…How?"

Another pause. Then:

"Same as the workers?"

I gripped my beer. I already knew. Kelley disconnected. He

didn't look at me. Just stood up, finished his drink, and grabbed his coat.

"What happened?" I asked.

Kelley exhaled through his nose.

"There was a shooting downtown." He was using his cop voice now—short sentences, no emotion.

"Fatality?"

He nodded. "Yeah."

I already knew. I just didn't want to say it.

"You said... 'same as the girls.'" My voice was tight. "What did you mean?"

Kelley stopped at the door and turned back.

"The gun caliber was the same."

I felt a dull pressure behind my ribs. I set my glass down and took a slow breath. "Anything else?"

Kelley stared at me for a long second.

Then he said:

"It was your new friend Carlton."

And then he was gone.

**14**

———————

Since I started looking for Kathy, four murders had happened. No one knew where she was, what she was doing, or if she was in danger. The man who had been paying me to find her was now dead.

There was no real reason to keep going except, since I started looking, four people had died.

I was closing up for the night. The bar was empty, and I dimmed the lights while I wiped things down. I had forgotten to lock the front door and went to fix the deadbolt when I saw movement in the shadows.

The Caretaker stepped inside like he'd always been there.

"Mr. Duffy, do you have time to share a Courvoisier with me?" He nodded toward the bar.

"I'll have a Jim Beam with you," I said. I locked the door and kept the lights low.

He removed his bowler and draped his coat neatly over a barstool. His gray suit was still sharply pressed and unwrinkled. A narrow burgundy tie completed the look.

"You know about Carlton." It wasn't a question.

"Yeah. The guy dies the afternoon I talk to him. I don't like coincidences."

"Doubtful that coincidence had anything to do with it," The Caretaker said. "Are you willing to stay with this?"

He raised his eyebrows and looked at me. Before I could speak, he continued.

"You would now be working for me. The pay will be $75,000."

I gave that some thought. The money would come in handy. Getting killed for it wouldn't.

"I don't know, Dush. This really ain't my thing. Besides, I thought you got me for Carlton. What's your interest?"

His face tightened, lips pressing together in thought.

"I had some financial interest in Carlton. A small consultant's fee, if you will. More of a tribute, really." He paused to sip his cognac. "More important to me is that I can't let people eliminate my associates. It is bad business. And some may get the wrong impression."

I let that sink in.

"So, if I can find Kathy or I can find who's behind the murders—then what?"

"Then that will be enough."

"And you're not expecting me to handle any kind of, uh... revenge?"

"Of course not," he said smoothly. He took another sip, holding the glass like it was an extension of his hand.

"But if I find them... someone else will, right?"

He didn't answer. Just turned the glass slightly, watching the liquid move.

I exhaled. If your actions get someone else murdered, aren't you complicit?

The Caretaker finally looked up, his tone conversational, almost friendly.

"I could get someone else to do this, you know," he said, motioning around the bar. "But it would be... unfortunate to see all of this change."

I watched him take another sip, his eyes scanning the room. He didn't have to say more.

"How did you know about that?" I asked.

"I make it my business to know what my associates are up against. It's important for my efforts."

I didn't respond right away. What the hell was I doing? Kelley was right. Shit, he was always right. I was an average prizefighter, a former human services counselor, and now a bar owner barely keeping his head above water. I wasn't a private eye. I wasn't a thug. I wasn't a superhero.

How the hell did I end up here?

Years ago, someone kidnapped the daughter of a woman on my caseload. The mother was a mess, addicted and desperate, and she begged me to find her kid. She said they were going to kill her. I thought she was crazy. I did nothing.

Days later, she was dead.

On cue, Al waddled out from his alcove. He lifted his head and barked twice.

Like the karmic force that he was, he reminded me. Walanda had made me take him before she went off to county jail. I hadn't wanted him, but I was stuck with him. Then she got killed, and somehow, we were still together.

It reminded me that sometimes, you don't get to choose what you take on.

I went and found Walanda's daughter back then. I busted up a child prostitution ring. That girl—now a social worker—drops by the bar every year around Thanksgiving. Every year, she thanks me for saving her life. A couple of times, her cousins, all gangbangers, helped me out and came to my rescue because of what I did. They let me know they'd never forget.

I let those memories settle over me.

"Duffy?"

The Caretaker's voice pulled me back.

I looked at him.

"I'll do it," I said.

**15**

———

Reno's friend was named Jack DeRossi. He came into the bar around 11, just as I was setting up. He was tall, maybe six-two, with wavy dark brown hair swept back, a prominent nose, and good teeth. His sharp features and Ralph Lauren gold golf shirt gave him the look of a guy who spent his mornings at the gym and his afternoons closing deals.

"Duff?" he said, like we were already friends. "Reno said you wanted to see me?"

"Uh yeah," I said. I was hoping Reno had prepped him so I wouldn't have to explain much.

"Platinum Experience? You're looking for a referral code? I can hook you up." He said it like he was offering a VIP membership to an exclusive golf club. There was no hesitation and no furtive looks around the room.

"Yeah, yeah, that's what I'm reaching out for," I said.

"You're gonna love it. These girls are top-tier. I mean, top shelf. And here's the crazy part—they know what they're doing. I mean, really know. And they'll do just about anything."

His excitement was electric, like a guy who just test-drove a

Ferrari. He wiped the corners of his mouth with his thumb and forefinger. He wore a wedding ring.

"How does it work? I, uh… I haven't done anything like this before." I let my words trail off, making it seem like I was just dipping my toes into the water.

"Piece of cake. Just a few things to keep the riff-raff out."

I wondered what exactly qualified someone as riff-raff in his world.

"You call or email. They'll ask for your code. Then you get a call back. You can let them assign you someone, or you can **request** someone specific—or, you know, a couple, if that's your thing. Then they'll give you an address, a time. That's it. Easy."

"You can request someone?"

"Yeah. It's all referral-based. The girl can say no—she might not be available, or she might not be taking new clients, whatever."

"You ever hear of Kathy Sullivan?"

I felt a twitch in my gut just saying her name.

"You kidding? She's my go-to. I mean, I spread it around, but she's my regular."

His face lit up like a guy talking about his favorite steakhouse.

"Man, she's got a killer body. Flat abs, toned thighs, perfect tits—shaved into a little heart."

The twitch in my gut turned into something worse.

"And shit, she knows what she's doing. Slips a finger here and there at just the right time when she's down there. Lets you make a mess all over her."

I forced myself to nod. "Wow."

"This shit ain't cheap, though. Fifteen hundred gets you in

the door. Then, it's à la carte. You get so turned on, you don't even care. I came out five grand lighter one time."

"Five grand…"

"Worth every penny." He nodded, eyes wide. "And honestly? It's good for my marriage."

That one threw me. "How's that?"

"Keeps me out of trouble. I stick to the pros, no drama, no emotional mess. Keeps the wife happy."

Jack DeRossi, master of rationalization.

"Yeah, man. Makes sense," I said, even though it made no sense at all.

"Duffy, you won't regret it. Trust me."

He scribbled a code on a coaster and slid it across the bar.

XXXKS&U.

Triple X. Kathy's initials. And you. Cute.

Jack took out a business card and placed it next to the coaster.

"By the way, if you ever think about selling this place, let me know. I'm in real estate."

Jack DeRossi, Agent. Integrity Properties.

I smirked at the name.

"I'll keep that in mind, Jack."

"You calling Kathy tonight?"

He sounded like a guy pushing me to test-drive a sports car.

"Yeah," I said. "Why not?"

I wasn't sure if I meant it. But I pocketed the coaster anyway.

**16**

___________

Something wasn't right. If DeRossi was still able to get ahold of Kathy for sex, why couldn't The Caretaker or Cusano? Could she just be in business for clients but avoiding her, I don't know, "management"?

There was no putting it off.

I had to try to go see Kathy and talk to her. The only way to get to her was to pay for a... a... um... session? Date? Rendezvous? I didn't like the pretense of calling for what was supposed to be sex, but as I thought about it more, it felt more honorable to call her to make an appointment for paid sex than just to have a chat. It was kind of ironic when the more honorable thing to do was to call her under the guise of sex rather than just looking for answers.

Something else made me twitch.

She'd have to remember me, right? It had been more than a decade, and we were just teenagers, but still—would she? And if she didn't, so what? Why did I care?

I wasn't sure I did, but I was having some sort of emotional response to it.

Maybe a decade of professional sex and exposure to who knows how many men would warp her memory. And what was it going to be like? Would she think I was there for sex? How icky would that be? Was there a history of former lovers lapsing into a pay-for-sex relationship with their exes-turned-escorts years after they split up?

Would she be embarrassed? Ashamed? Maybe she was comfortable in her life now but wouldn't be comfortable displaying it to someone she used to be in love with... even as an adolescent. Or maybe she looked back at our adolescent relationship as stupid and silly. Maybe she thought I was stupid and silly and maybe, in some twisted way, I had set her on this path.

I don't think I had that kind of power.

I fished the coaster DeRossi gave me with the code on it and called the number. Then, I waited for the callback.

It came in less than 15 minutes.

"This is Kathy. You called for an appointment?"

My mouth went dry.

"Yes."

"Your name, please."

"John," I said. I couldn't believe I came up with the name "John."

"John, will you be paying with a credit card or cash?"

"Cash."

"Very good. I have an opening at 8:15. Would that work for you?"

"Yup."

"Terrific. John, my space is right next to the park. I'm at 15 Jefferson, fourth floor, apartment six. I look forward to meeting you." Her voice was older than I remembered. It was smooth, confident, and only held traces of what I remembered.

I got a strange feeling.

I had an hour. I decided to get my questions straight. Wording was important, and I needed to convey whatever it was I was trying to get to without being judgmental.

"Are you okay?"

"Are you in any physical danger?"

"People you work for—no, work with—are concerned that you've been out of touch. Can you contact them?"

I guess that's what I needed to know.

That's what I was hired for.

The Duffy questions like "How the hell did you wind up like this?" "What happened to you?" "Did it have anything to do with me?"—those would all have to go unanswered.

I was in front of her building at 8:10. I took a deep breath and went in. It was a classic old brownstone that overlooked the park. There wasn't a red light out in front, and the stairway walls weren't covered in red velvet. There was no elevator, and it dawned on me that her clientele would have to have a modicum of decent cardiovascular conditioning to climb these stairs.

Maybe that was her way of selecting and eliminating some clientele.

I knocked gently on the door. I was incredibly self-conscious. The anxiety ran through all of my veins.

"One minute," she softly said from a distance behind the door.

I swallowed. I heard her undo a deadbolt and turn the knob.

"Hi, John. Come on in." She made confident eye contact. It was sexy in its own way, like she was 100% present in why you were there. "Can I get you a drink?"

She was beautiful: platinum blonde hair, subtle makeup, bright red lipstick, and crystal blue eyes. She smiled at me and motioned me to a large distressed leather couch. She wore form-fitting faded blue jeans and a men's-style white shirt with the first three buttons undone. You could see nicely formed breasts hinted at by the blouse. Her skin was lightly tanned, and she smelled of good soap and light cologne.

She was gorgeous.

"Bourbon?" "Wine?" "Beer?"

"I'd love a bourbon," I said. That was for sure.

"Maker's okay?"

I nodded.

I realized, in my anxiety, I had forgotten why I came here. Certainly, she didn't recognize me, or she was playing it off in the most convincing of ways.

She turned and handed me my bourbon. It was in a heavy, very masculine rocks glass. She had a white wine in a long-stemmed wine glass. She sat next to me on the couch and lightly placed her hand on my thigh.

My mouth went dry.

She wore bright red, three-inch pumps—the only overt nod to sexiness in her wardrobe.

"You seem a bit nervous, John. I know this is your first time with me. I'm guessing it's your first time with a pro?" She smiled a welcoming and comforting smile. She leaned into me a bit and ran a perfectly manicured index finger lightly across my cheek.

I looked at her. Her eyes were incredible. Her lips were perfect. And yet, something felt… off.

Then her hand traveled up my thigh and over the crotch of my jeans.

"Clearly, you're not too nervous," she chuckled, looking up at me with wide eyes.

I wasn't sure I could pull this off. I mean, the questioning part. She was that powerful.

"Um, can we stop—I mean, stop before we get going?" I said. I was back to being a nervous 18-year-old. I took a long sip of the bourbon. It went down hard and burned.

"Sure, John. We can take our time. No need to rush." "Um, I came here under false pretenses. Um..." She didn't let me finish.

"Don't tell me you're a fucking cop!" She stood up abruptly from the couch. All the smooth erotic sweetness was gone. In that instant, it became apparent she really was a working girl.

"No, no, no... I'm not a cop." I paused. I looked at her closely, and it came over me. Something wasn't right. Against my better judgment, I asked.

"You don't remember me?"

She looked at me like I was crazy.

"From Crawford High? Duffy?"

She gave me a blank stare.

I looked closer. No scar on her chin. Maybe a tad too tall. The posture and the mannerisms were all wrong.

"You're not her, are you?"

A look came over her—part anger, part embarrassment.

"You gotta go. No charge. You gotta go."

She reached into a drawer, pulled out a gun, and pointed it at me.

"Get the fuck out of here!"

I left.

## 17

They let me go after a few more of the same type of questions. When I asked why they were looking for Kathy, they declined to say.

They were federal. What made something a federal crime? Kidnapping? Counterfeiting? Threats against elected officials? Interstate something-or-other? I was going to have to ask Kelley. He wouldn't like it, but it was something I needed to know. When I got back to the bar, The Foursome—Pasquale, Kelley, Kim, and Patti—were in, along with the new couple with the vegetarian wife. Billy had things covered.

Al was asleep on the bar at the far end. He had probably climbed up the boxes in the kitchen and made the two-foot leap. It defied physics, but I had quit trying to figure out how he did it. No one minded. An 85-pound hound asleep on the bar wasn't out of the ordinary anymore.

"Thanks, Billy. All good?" I asked as I got behind the bar.

"Yeah. The vegetarian asked for a vegetarian Reuben. I had her walk me through it." He rolled his eyes.

"They come in pretty regularly. Did she refer to it as a 'Sueben' and then clap her hands?"

"Yep."

"That's her."

"Duff, stock is kind of low. We're gonna be out of Narragansett soon."

I nodded and tried not to show any response. Thankfully, The Foursome distracted me.

"The crocodile has teeth on the bottom, whereas the alligator has teeth on the top," Rocco said.

Billy glanced at him. "Okay if I go?"

"You don't want to hear this one play out?"

Billy smiled, grabbed his keys, and headed out.

"Aren't alligators bigger?" TC asked.

"Sure. They got the teeth on the top. Means they can eat more," Jerry Number Two said.

"Huh? How does that work?" TC said.

"You ever try to eat with just your bottom teeth? It's very hard," Jerry Number One said.

I pictured it in my head. It wasn't making much sense, but before I could say anything, Jeopardy! came on, and Pasquale perked up.

Ken Jennings read the question—er, answer.

"This Civil War general was famous for his march on Atlanta."

"Patton!" TC blurted.

"God, you're a moron," Rocco said. "It's Grant."

"No, it isn't Grant," Pasquale chimed in. "I can't think of his name… Shit, what is it?"

"Mr. Jeopardy big-shot champion," Rocco muttered.

"Custard! It was Custard!" TC shouted.

The bar stopped and stared at him.

"Custard. You know, later he was famous for his restaurant—'The Last Stand.' People don't realize he was a Civil War hero." TC beamed with pride.

The door swung open, and Kelley slid past The Foursome like a man avoiding a minefield. He grumbled something under his breath about "more useless trivia" and landed on his usual barstool.

"Kelley will know," Rocco said. "Kell, what Civil War guy led the march on Atlanta?"

I slid Kelley a Bud Light.

"Sherman," he said without looking up.

"You sure?" TC asked. "I'm almost positive it was Custard. You know, the restaurant guy."

Kelley glanced at TC for a split second.

"Oh boy, here we go," he muttered.

I had to tell him about Kathy and my newest findings, and I knew he would be pissed. Still, the information was relevant to his own investigation—or at least his department's.

"You're not going to like this," I started. "But I think I've got to tell you anyway."

"Go ahead, General Custard. How much worse can it get?"

I took a breath. "I made an appointment to see Kathy."

Kelley narrowed his eyes. "And?"

I exhaled. "It wasn't her."

He just looked at me.

"Seriously. At first, I thought it was, but I was nervous and not thinking straight. Then I realized it wasn't her. No scar on her chin. Someone was doing their best to look like her."

"What did you say to her?"

"I confronted her. She got really weird, pissed off—then pulled a gun on me and told me to leave."

Kelley stared at me for a long moment, his jaw tightening. "Sounds like prom was more fun for you."

I ignored him. "That's not all of it, Kell."

His eyes flicked upward. "Jesus. What now?"

"When I got back to my car, two federal agents were waiting for me."

Kelley blinked. "Feds?"

"Yeah. Pulled me into their car, started asking about Kathy."

Kelley set down his beer. "Jesus, Duff."

"I told them what I knew, and they let me go."

He took another sip. I could see him turning it over in his head."Kelley, what is it?" I asked.

"I don't know," he said, still thinking. He took another sip, then looked at me.

"But I do know one thing."

"What's that?"

He gave me a long look.

"You're so far over your fuckin' head, you're in another time zone."

---

## 18

I didn't get any sleep. The dogs were up and down and I kept turning things over in my head. If I had a nickel for every time Kelley told me I was in over my head I could probably get the bar out of debt.

Maybe.

Between the bar business, the mess with Kathy and the accumulating dead bodies, my head was spinning. Actually, I had that weird feeling like I wasn't in the right body or something- things were just too out of order and nothing was lining up like it was supposed to. I've gotten this feeling enough over the course of my life but with everything going on lately it had gone to another level.

I did what I had always done when I felt out of sorts-I went to the boxing gym. Since I was 14, ravaged with acne and as insecure as a teenage boy could be, the boxing gym was my solace. Smitty taught me to box and through that process without a word being said I learned a lot more. I learned what true toughness was by getting into the ring, scared to death, taking punches to face and learning that I could take it and come back to it again the next day. It is hard to explain in today's world how simple and important this lesson is.

I also learned what hard work was. It became something far more than an abstraction because of boxing. I had to work hard to get better, to learn to move, to learn to block, and to learn to fake and strike. If I didn't work hard and didn't progress, I'd just keep getting beaten up. There is really only one trajectory in boxing: you either got better, or you found something else to do. Or you became one of those fake guys who hung around hitting the bags and strutting around like you were a fighter, but you and everyone else knew you really weren't.

Fighters fight. It is pretty simple.

Nowadays, I taught this more than I did it, which made me uneasy. I didn't preach anything about the inner meanings of boxing because Smitty didn't. It was something new kids and experienced fighters needed to learn on their own from their experience. You couldn't just tell them about it.

It followed the same logic as living; at least, for me, it did. I looked at life and how it unfolded through the eyes of a fighter. Sometimes that concerned me. Maybe life isn't a fight; maybe it isn't about taking punches and keeping at it; maybe it is something softer and gentler.

That just hasn't been my experience. Life jabbed pretty well, often followed it up with a hard cross and a finishing hook. Sometimes you slip and shield it; sometimes you take it on the chin; and sometimes it puts you on your ass. Other times, you countered life, stood it up, and made it take a step back and get on the defensive.

There was a cold and steady mid-November rain coming down in sheets, and I ran from the lot into the Y to minimize getting soaked. As I headed down to the basement, I immediately picked up the steady rhythms of the bags being hit, the slight vibration from the heavy bags swaying and shaking the ceiling, and the leathery, sweaty scent that rose from the room.

It was a busy night. Trevon was in the ring sparring with a slightly younger, less experienced kid. Lorenzo was getting his own work in, doing some focused heavy bag work. He was deep into it, and his left hooks rattled the whole gym. The guy had something in his hands and could really hit. Malik was winding down with a skipping rope, Piggy was blasting the heavy bag, alternating left and right body shots, and a couple of the other boxers were there, all in motion.

Trevon and Lorenzo set the tone. When a couple of the best in the gym were working hard and focused, the sentiment bled throughout the gym. It was magic, and I loved it. The fact that the two of them were bonded and that 'Zo had such a metamorphosis in his life just made me smile. It wasn't an overstatement to say he turned Trevon's life around.

The bells sounded to end the round, and the noise subsided for sixty seconds. Lorenzo and I bumped fists, and Trevon called to me from his corner in the ring. The rest of the fighters gave me quick hellos before they went back to work.

I went to the office for a quick check of what had come in on the email and the phone.

It was Smitty's office, and I had left it in the same condition and order since he left. It didn't feel right to change anything around, and I didn't know if that was because of a deep-seated hope that he was coming back or that I didn't feel worthy to take his place.

The Y still had an archaic landline phone system, and the

gym office actually still had an answering machine with Smitty's message.

It went: "You've reached the Crawford Y Boxing Club. Leave a message."

That was it. That was Smitty.

There were three hangups and then a message.

"Duff, this is Carl from Top Star. We'd like to know if Lorenzo would like to fight for the IBF title January 15. Lewis has a non-mandatory. Lorenzo beat him in the amateurs, and it would make for good hype. The network wants it, and the money would be good. Call me."

I did like they did in the movies; I just looked at the receiver.

I played the message again.

I had heard it correctly.

The heavyweight title. Holy shit.

The fuckin' heavyweight title.

Champions often have to fight a mandatory challenger who is currently ranked in the top ten or twenty. Lewis just won the title, so he had the option of fighting a non-mandatory bout for his first title defense. They saw Lorenzo as an easy bout, and the fact that Lorenzo beat him in the amateurs would make for some marketing possibilities. Amateur boxing is a whole different game, and the fact that Zo beat him in the amateurs didn't mean much, but the average fan didn't know that.

I let Zo finish up his workout. When he did, he came over to the office, covered in sweat and still breathing hard.

"'Sup D?" he said and bumped my fist with his. He still had his wraps on and began to unravel them.

"Something I want you to hear," I said.

Zo furrowed his brow and looked confused.

I hit the answering machine. We listened in silence.

Zo's eyebrows went up, and then he looked at me.

"The title? The fuckin' heavyweight title?" he said, his voice going up an octave.

"You wanna do it? Gonna be some work, you know," I said.

"Hellll yeah!" Zo stretched hell into a bunch of syllables.

"Let's do it!" I said. "I'll get the details. Tomorrow we map out a training camp, and we get after it, okay?" I said.

"Helllll yeah!"

**19**

———————

Zo and I agreed to meet the next day to map out the strategy for training. We had twelve weeks—just about perfect.

We'd need to set up strength training, cardio work, nutrition, and, of course, quality sparring. That meant traveling to New York or even Philly to get rounds in with guys who fought like Lewis.

The problem was money.

Top-tier guys like Lewis had a budget. They could afford to pay sparring partners, hire strength coaches and nutritionists, and get a stipend to live on while they trained. Lorenzo had me, a failing bar, and his day job at the agency that supported Trevon. But that was okay. Jack Dempsey didn't have a nutritionist, and he did just fine.

Still, the championship money was life-changing, and the manager's cut could save the bar. I told myself that wasn't my focus, but I'd be lying if I said it didn't cross my mind.

"Look, Zo, it's pouring out. Take my coat and hat. I've got a spare here," I said. "Can't have a title contender catching pneumonia."

"Nah, D, I'll be chill."

"First lesson of training camp—you do what the coach says."

He grinned, wide and easy.

"A'ight." He took the jacket, holding it up. "*Elvis On Tour*? Not exactly Drake or Fiddy."

"Exactly."

"Kickin' it old school. Appreciate it, D. We'll link up tomorrow?"

I nodded. This was the biggest thing that had ever happened to him. Just getting a title shot was life-changing. But winning the heavyweight championship of the world? That was something else entirely.

He called out to Trevon, who grabbed his duffel and fell in beside him. They headed out together.

I stood in the doorway and watched them go.

Lorenzo came into the gym a punk. He represented everything I hated about the streets—lazy, loud, careless. I beat his ass in the ring, threw him out, and figured that was the end of it.

But he came back.

I never understood why.

Then he found Trevon. The kid had been through hell. Mom was a sixteen-year-old addict, and every boyfriend she had abused Tre. He lived in a group home, bouncing between foster care and shelters.

For some reason, Zo took to him. Maybe he saw himself in Tre. Maybe he was making up for his own past mistakes. Either way, they bonded. They became like father and son.

Zo even put his career on hold for Trevon. A year ago, he

backed out of a career-making fight because it fell on the same night as Tre's first amateur bout. Zo promised to be in his corner. He didn't hesitate.

Now, karma was paying him back with a title shot.

I leaned against the office doorway, taking it all in. Sometimes life made sense when you stepped back and looked at it.

Other times, it was a goddamn mess.

But this? This was good.

I sat at Smitty's desk, leaned back, and put my feet up.

"Smitty, don't let me screw this up," I muttered.

And just like that, I could hear his voice in my head.

"Son, don't worry about screwin' up. You're gonna do that plenty without even tryin'. Just go do what you gotta do the best you can."

God, I missed him.

Nothing felt solid anymore. Nothing felt *together* anymore. I wasn't the kid in the ring looking up at Smitty for guidance—I was the guy in the corner now. The one responsible for the safety net.

I wasn't sure I was up for it.

Then the screaming started.

"DUFFY! DUFFY!"

It was a panicked, high-pitched voice. It was Trevon.

I was on my feet before he even made it to the doorway.

"Tre, what's up?"

He was out of breath, soaked from the rain, wild-eyed.

"C'mon! Lorenzo's been shot! He's in the parking lot! You gotta do somethin'!"

**20**

———————

I called 911 and sprinted up the stairs with Trevon right behind me, taking two and three at a time. His breathing was heavy, but it wasn't from running stairs. I knew because mine was the same.

Lorenzo was just outside the door. Fat Eddie, the locker room attendant, was kneeling beside him, pressing hard on his chest. Blood pooled around Lorenzo's side, spreading across the wet pavement.

"Duffy, take over," Eddie said, his voice tight.

I dropped to my knees, putting my hands over Lorenzo's wound and pressing down, but warm blood seeped between my fingers.

"C'mon, Zo. C'mon," Trevon stared at us with tears running down his face.

Sirens cut through the night. Two police cars and an ambulance screeched to a stop. Two EMTs jumped out, moving fast. One was tall and wiry, wearing an EMT baseball cap. His voice was calm but direct.

"Let us through," he said, not asking.

I stepped back, my hands covered in Zo's blood.

"Single gunshot wound to the upper left chest, massive bleeding," the wiry EMT called out to his partner, a muscular Black guy with a thick beard. They moved fast, securing Lorenzo onto a gurney. No wasted movements, no hesitation.

Trevon grabbed my sleeve. "Is he—"

"They've got him," I said, more to convince myself than him.

The EMTs loaded Lorenzo into the ambulance. The wiry one climbed into the back while the bearded driver slammed the door shut and hit the sirens. They peeled out, running the light at State Street.

A uniformed cop stepped up. No hat, perfect fade, muscles straining against his sleeves. His name tag read *Martinez*.

"Who called this in?"

"Me," I said, voice flat.

"You see it happen?"

"No. Trevon was with him." I motioned toward Tre.

Martinez turned. "You were with him?"

Tre nodded. His face was blank, eyes glassy. I think he was in shock.

"What did you see?"

Trevon lifted a shaky hand and pointed toward the streetlamp. "There. The guy stepped out and shot once."

"You get a look at him?"

"He was wearing a black hoodie and jeans with tan work boots. White guy, medium build. He shot and ran."

"Which way?"

"Same way the ambulance went. Up State Street."

Martinez glanced at the dark street, processing. "Anything stand out about him?"

Tre blinked, his mind working to replay what happened. "He had… a limp. Like a hamstring thing."

Martinez frowned. "Hamstring thing?"

Trevon nodded. "Like he hurt it a while ago, but it was still messing with him."

An unmarked Impala pulled up. Kelley stepped out, wearing his CPD-issued windbreaker and baseball hat, soaked from the rain. He ignored me at first, walking straight to where Lorenzo had been lying.

Martinez filled him in. "Shooter came from behind the telephone pole. White male, dark clothes, hoodie, work boots. Ran with a limp."

Kelley nodded, then turned to Trevon. "You okay?"

Tre nodded, but his face said otherwise.

"Did the shooter say anything?" Kelley pressed. "Do anything weird?"

Trevon's lips parted like he was about to speak, then stopped. He shook his head.

"How'd he hold the gun?"

Trevon lifted his hand, forming a finger gun, tilting it sideways, parallel to the ground. The way the gang guys did.

Kelley's eyes flicked to me. "You see anything?"

"No. I was still inside. He was wearing my *Elvis in Concert* jacket and my Yankees cap."

Kelley's jaw tensed. His eyes stayed locked on me.

"So this was meant for you."

A lump formed in my throat. I exhaled and nodded.

"Yeah."

## 21

—————

I followed Kelley and the ambulance to the hospital. Trevon came along, and even though he was too young to be dealing with something this heavy, something told me he needed to come. I was sick with fear and guilt. I couldn't shake the thought that the bullet was meant for me. Instead, it hit a young man on the verge of his dream. A dream everyone in this business wanted.

There was a lot of blood. Lorenzo had no response to anything. While I did chest compressions, his face stayed vacant. It wasn't good. It wasn't good at all.

Kelley pulled into the emergency lane, but I had to circle around to the parking lot. Trevon hadn't said a word. His breathing was shallow, his eyes locked forward. Lorenzo was his whole world. His savior. The man who gave him hope and a reason to keep going. Now, this. No kid should have to process something like this.

"C'mon, we'll go in and wait. He'll probably go right into surgery, so we won't know anything for a while," I said. Trevon followed but didn't respond.

The hospital smell, that antiseptic mixed with lemon or pine or whatever, hit me the second we went through the revolving door. There was a grand lobby at St. Mark's now with large waiting rooms, a kiosk snack bar, and rocking chairs. Making a hospital look like a Marriott didn't change your reason for being there or make it any better to me. It was almost insulting that they did it to market the place.

Kelley was talking to a nurse or some sort of medical person behind a glass partition. We were about 25 feet away. From that distance, it looked like he asked a question or two, then he nodded, took out a notebook, and made a quick note. We approached him.

"Is there anything to know?" I asked.

Kelley blew out a deep breath.

"He coded in the ambulance. They got him back really quick, so they don't think it was long enough for brain damage," he said. He took a quick glance at Trevon and pursed his lips. He took me by the elbow and guided me out of Trevon's hearing distance.

"It doesn't look good. They brought him right into surgery. His chest was all torn up, he lost a lot of blood, and the whole medical team had dour looks on their faces. I'd be ready for..." He didn't finish the sentence. He didn't have to. We stood there in silence.

There was nothing left to say.

Over the course of your lifespan, you aren't faced with true life-and-death situations all that often; maybe, if you're lucky, it is a handful of times. The first time it comes, usually a grandparent or someone similar, and it shakes your world. Even if the person was sick, you always, I don't know, expected them to be there. The permanence of death hits you in waves; like you don't get it, and then it punches you and lets you know the person you loved is gone, not coming back, not now, not soon, not ever. It isn't hard to see how, if religion wasn't right with its assertion, man would come up with it as a means to cope.

"Trevon's probably going to have to go back to his apartment," Kelley interrupted my reverie. "They got rules on being out all night without their guardian."

Their guardian. It dawned on me that Lorenzo was that in every meaning of the word.

"Yeah, you're right," I said.

"I can run him over," Kelley said.

I walked Trevon over to Kelley and explained the situation. He looked disappointed, but as a kid in the system, he'd been conditioned not to protest. I bumped fists with him and resisted the urge to tell him everything was going to be alright. I did my best not to lie to people I cared about, and just because they were young didn't give me an excuse.

I looked around the waiting room and tried to strategize how I was going to wait here. I had spent a night in a hospital when Hymie was getting ready to pass. He was my unofficial Jewish grandfather who looked after me at the clinic. He founded the place, was its main funder, and liked the way I worked; that is, I put people first and all the red tape second or lower on the list. He begged me to do my paperwork so I would stay out of trouble, but I failed him there. When he was around, he ran interference between me and Claudia.

When Hymie died, I knew things would change. Claudia's power became unrestrained. My outburst at the clinic came after a series of things in my life in that moment, but it was also brewing inside me, and I guessed it was as much about the place going to shit after Hymie than it was anything else.

I found an empty waiting room down the hall from the main emergency room waiting room and parked myself in a vinyl semi-easy chair that wasn't as comfortable as it was supposed to look. The TV was on CNN, and the anchor with the slicked-back hair and chiseled jaw was reporting on the president-elect's comments about immigrants. I scrambled for the remote and flipped the channel. I landed on SportsCenter, and the guy on this alternative with the slicked-back hair and the chiseled jaw was reporting about the intricacies of the college playoff system. I saw an earlier version of this same story at the bar this morning.

My mind drifted. Hospital memories come back when your nervous system picks up the same smells, sounds, and lights. They trigger the feelings you had the other times you were in the hospital. My muscles tightened, and I struggled with trying not to feel. It didn't work. Suppression never did.

I was too restless to sit still.

I took a walk and found myself heading back toward the emergency room. It wasn't as crowded as it was, but there were still a dozen or so folks waiting. None looked happy, and the room was mostly quiet, with CNN echoing in the background.

"Mr. Duffy." It came from behind the glass at admissions.

"Yes?"

"Are you the next of kin for Mr. Cordero?"

"Um, no, um—is he all right?"

She looked away.

"I have to identify the next of kin," she said, not making eye contact.

"Is he gone?"

"Do you know the next of kin?" She ignored my question.

A tall, thin guy with a lab coat opened her door and stuck his head in and said, "Time of death for Cordero, 2:38 a.m."

And I knew.

## 22

————

The feeling was the feeling I've known before. For me, it starts off as fear.

It is the sense that the worst that could happen happened. You thought maybe things weren't as bad and that you were exaggerating in your mind. That things will be okay, that this is just your mind running away from you. Then the news comes, and you realize really bad things can happen.

The worst can happen.

When you're a kid, you don't believe it.

Then life gives you an education. It is an education we all get. Some get it very early in life, and it has to change how everything is filtered after that. The child can't understand and is forever altered. When it happens to an adult, the same process goes on, just in different ways.

Life can be lost. People die. They are gone forever.

Maybe that's where religion comes from. The belief is so hard to accept you have to create something bigger than you to make the pieces fit.

Maybe.

This time it was my fault. It was because of me. Someone wanted me dead because of what I was looking into, and Lorenzo was in the wrong place at the wrong time, and he was dressed like me.

He was a troubled kid. A bad kid who improbably turned it around. He became a man. He became a father to Trevon and changed their lives. Now, Trevon was a casualty and will never be the same. He will have that unreal feeling, but he'll have it as a teenager who just lost the man who made him whole. The man who made him worth something. The man he loved.

I almost threw up.

I was going to have to tell Trevon. I had my own grief, and the thought of the kid and how it would affect him was too much for me to even process.

I don't know about all that shit about stages of grief, but as I sat there, something else was welling up in me. I recognized it because I had known it my whole life. Some would call it anger, but that didn't touch it. It was something more than that.

It narrowed my vision. It caused tension in my head and shoulders, and it made the blood pulse in my veins. It was anger plus that negative energy of wanting to strike back at a world that dealt cards like this. Dealt shit like this to me my whole life and now dealt them to a blameless kid like Trevon. He didn't deserve this. Lorenzo didn't deserve this.

I knew in a very short period of time that someone was going to have to pay for this. It was an out-of-balance equation right now that needed to be fixed. Someone was going to have to pay.

There was no doubt.

I drove to the institution that oversaw Trevon's supported apartment. It was down Academy Road and was a series of cottages, a main building, a school, a gym, and the requisite softball field and antiseptic playground equipment. Just looking at it and knowing this was where kids went when their parents, neighborhoods, culture—whatever—couldn't give them what they needed and gave them a whole world of what they didn't need.

Abuse, neglect, pain.

I went into the building marked "Administration." It was a nondescript lobby with a glassed-in section where a couple of women chatted away, oblivious to my presence at the window.

I tapped on the glass lightly to get their attention.

An overweight woman with ridiculous multicolored nails, a nose ring, and bright red lipstick slid the glass over.

"Can I help you?" she said without a trace of notion that she wanted to do anything of the sort.

"I'm Duffy Dombrowski. I run the gym that Trevon goes to. I need to speak to him. It is really important."

She glanced at her partner, another twenty-something with long straight hair and a pale complexion. She was wearing an oversized light gray sweatsuit and was drinking something from Starbucks.

"We can't divulge information about the people we support," the first one said.

"The people you support? Never mind. It is important. Lorenzo, his coach, he…" I couldn't say it out loud. "I don't want Trevon to hear it from somebody else."

She frowned like I was so unfortunately ignorant.

"I'm sorry, sir. We can't."

I wasn't in the mood.

"Look, do some fucking thinking for a change. Lorenzo died. Did you hear what I fucking said? I don't want the kid to hear it from somebody else. Now, get him for me." It came out a lot louder and way more aggressive than I intended.

She sat back in her chair, and her eyes went wide.

"Call 911!" the other said.

She did.

This wasn't going to help anything.

I left.

**23**

———————

I didn't even wait to get home. I needed to take action, not just to solve this thing but to get my mind straight by doing something. If I let myself think of Lorenzo or Trevon, especially Trevon, I just couldn't deal with things at all. It wasn't a time for ambivalence; it was a time for action. That's what I thought, and even though I wasn't sure what that action would be, it was the direction I had to go.

Sitting around and feeling wasn't an option.

When it came to understanding crime, there were a few places I could go.

There was Kelley, but with Kelley came judgment, hard commands to leave it alone, and sometimes interference. Honestly, it was usually good advice but not advice I wanted to take. Logic got in my way when I felt like this. It slowed me down, which many would argue was probably a good thing. I had to keep moving.

There was also the Caretaker, but I wasn't sure where he stood with this situation. He didn't talk a lot; he got me into this, but when I stopped to think about it all, it didn't add up—

or at least it didn't totally add up. First, he hires me, kind of puts himself as an intermediary, to help an acquaintance. When that man gets killed, he decides to keep me on the case. With his own coin. Fifty K is a large amount of money without a really specific reason. Sure, the Caretaker didn't want bad guys encroaching on his turf and all that, but would even the Caretaker make a point for out-of-pocket expenses that big?

I didn't think so.

Pasquale knew enough about the darker side of society, but he knew about it from the periphery, not from its center. He flirted with it by the nature of the strip club, but it didn't put him right in the center. There was also Reno, who also flirted with a crime lifestyle but nothing that would make him an insider. Nas, from the Port of Albany, might know something, but I didn't know him all that well, and something told me not to try him yet because I had nothing to barter.

That left Jack Daniels.

A retired Chicago detective, Jack knew crime and probably too well. She had paid the price for it and retired, and since then her retirement had been far from an idyllic existence. She—and yes, Jack was a she—and I teamed up one time when I was in her town, and someone kidnapped Al and a little girl with Down Syndrome. We got them both back safely, and the little girl loved her time with my floppy-eared buddy. Al had some indigestion and wound up vomiting, but that's what happens when you bite off four of a bad guy's digits.

"Daniels," was how Jack answered the phone.

"So sweet you are. Just such a lovely feminine ray of sunshine," I said.

"Oh good, it's Duffy. Undoubtedly looking for a favor in another one of his quid pro quo deals," she said.

"Quid pro quo? Is that even a thing?" I said.

"What do you want?" she said.

"Porn industry, sex trafficking, and the mafia—go!"

"Geez, Duf, I don't have a week…"

"They still running the porn and prostitution or has things like Mindfun, the internet, and Vegas made all the dirty things the nuns told me not to legit as IBM?"

"I'm sure you paid close attention to those nuns."

"More than you'd know."

Jack exhaled. It was part sigh and part fatigue.

"Okay, here goes. The money is mostly handled in a legit way. I'm sure you've read about Mindfun and its corporate squeaky clean Canadian offices. They've made it legit and are just serving a need and all that bullshit. They don't have any direct money lines that can track right to prostitution. All of that is handled by the people who supply content to them, but their content is how customers find out about their, uh, services. So they are at least middlemen."

"Trafficking?" I asked.

"Again, Mindfun doesn't traffic, but when they post videos or make contacts available for sex-for-pay, it is one step away from it. Who knows what money exchanges hands and what that money is really for when it is put on a receipt? That is, if there is a receipt."

"Do women in the life have it better than they used to?"

"Depends which women you're talking about. The top one percent probably live sensational lives if you don't mind people sticking body parts in you. The ones that are appearing in weird, abusive, non-consensual, awful videos or who are made to do shit they don't want to are still being treated worse than animals."

"Certainly worse than a basset hound we both know," I said.

"Duffy, I pray I'm reincarnated as a basset hound. That guy eats, shits, farts, and screws whatever he wants to when he wants to."

"You have such a way with words." I paused for a second. "So, how does organized crime benefit, and how could I get close to that?"

Silence.

A long silence.

"So you're not looking for all this info because you're taking a junior college course. You're not writing a magazine article or something like that?"

"Yeah, let's go with one of those," I said.

"It doesn't matter. You're gonna do what you're gonna do anyway." She sighed even harder than the last time. "As always, follow the money. The low-level scumbags, pimps, movie makers, internet content providers make the shit and either sell it or share it with someone who can do something with it. That asshole scumbag takes a cut or takes ownership for a below-market price and passes it on. It is basic economics, only with scum of the earth scumbags."

"So if I had content or a woman or…"

She didn't let me finish.

"No, no, no. Just no…" she said with more than a little desperation.

"I didn't say I was going to."

"You didn't have to. Duffy, it is a scummy business, and you couldn't fake it. You'll get caught, and by not nice people. Stay away from this."

I didn't say anything.

"Oh hell, what's the use? At least be careful. You'll have to find a buyer, a middleman, or a broker of some sort, and then, well, follow the money."

"Got it. Thanks, Jack."

"No point in me saying stay out of this, is there?"

"Thanks, Jack. I owe you."

"I know. I'm not holding my breath."

Then she hung up.

## 24

My head was spinning. Just a little too much of everything at too high a level for too long. I needed to be in something familiar, something that would steady and center me. I went to the bar. Lorenzo and then talking to Jack left me, I don't know—unsteady.

The afternoon group was in. Ky, Carl, and Sheena took up the corner of the bar. Coffees for Kyrone and Carl, and Sheena was sipping a Diet Coke with no ice. They were already into it and didn't acknowledge me when I walked by. That was fine by me, especially if they were doing their work.

Ky caught sight of me and walked over to talk to me down the bar.

"Sorry about your friend, man." He wasn't dramatic about it. Just those words, soft and sincere.

I nodded, not trusting my voice. He went back to the corner.

Billy came in from the kitchen with a case of Bud Light—I think it was the last one—in one hand and a bar towel over his shoulder. He gave me a look, and I gave him one back. Neither of us said it, but we both knew what the other was thinking.

"You hear?" he asked.

"Yeah," I said. "You okay?"

Billy set the case down gently. "He was good, Duff. You know? He didn't just work there. He gave a damn. Especially about that kid."

"Trevon."

"Yeah. Zo was like… I don't know. A real one. Not a talker, just a doer. The gym's not going to be the same."

I let that sit in the air for a minute. Then I told Billy I wasn't going to hang around; I wanted to get to the gym. He nodded. Billy didn't say anything else, but I could see the concern and emotion in his eyes.

The gym was quiet, and because it was a place that would be filled with noise later on, the quiet was more pronounced. I walked past the ring, past the heavy bags, and to the back where the lockers lined the wall.

Lorenzo's was still shut. The lock was old, but I remembered the combo. He gave it to me once when he got back to his apartment and thought he had left his phone there. He did, and I ran it over that night.

I turned the dial and popped it open.

A couple of pairs of wraps, bag gloves, a foul protector, a hoodie, a crumpled protein bar wrapper, and a spiral notebook with frayed corners.

The cover read: "Trevon Success Plan."

I flipped through it. It was more than just drills or exercises. It was detailed and structured, with pages of notes and motivational scribbles in the margins.

In the back pocket, there was something else. A folded piece of pink lined paper.

I opened it.

*Zo—*

*Thanks for helping me. I know it's dangerous. I'm scared, and I'm not sure what to do.*

*—Juanita.*

I stared at it. The name hit me like a body shot.

Juanita.

She was one of the murdered women. One of the ones killed in the beginning.

What the hell was Zo doing?

I folded the letter and slid it into my jacket pocket. As I did, my phone buzzed. I didn't recognize the number.

The text read:

*You're getting too close. Stay out of this.*

I put the phone away, zipped my jacket, and headed out. Whatever Lorenzo had been doing, it wasn't just training fighters.

And whatever I'd stumbled into, I wasn't backing off now.

**25**

———————

Trevon Shows Up at the Gym Beaten

I needed to go to the gym for a couple of reasons. One, it was where I'd gone to decompress since I was a zit-faced awkward kid at 14. I was goofy, a former karate guy, and when I got to the gym and learned that I had the guts to get in the ring, get beat up, and return, I learned a lot of things about myself.

I learned I wasn't a pussy. I know that's what the kids, or at least the woke kids, call toxic masculinity. For me, it taught that in life I could face shit and keep on coming. Maybe getting hit in the face really wasn't the best way to learn that, but it might be the realist. I saw something once on the history of college football about the fact that it was encouraged among school-age boys after the Civil War because the country thought our young men without war would be soft.

Harsh? Hell yeah. True?

I think so.

There's something different about boxing that's important.

It is just you. You don't have an offensive line or a halfback to block for you. You're a team. I think for me, well, I've never been one of those "go team" dudes. Not only that, I also felt that the guys who were "go teamy" were full of shit.

I'm guessing my lack of belief in such camaraderie kept me from buying into the whole concept. Boxing left you alone, by yourself, no one to block for you, no one to run interference. And when you get beat, it's all you, and everyone can see it.

Find me a good shrink, and I'll let them figure it out.

I've stopped trying.

The other reason I had to go to the gym was, whether I wanted it to be true or not, I was in charge. Lorenzo was gone, and I didn't have a number two.

There was the workout for the young boxers, and there was no one to run it. I wanted to be there for Trevon. Especially for Trevon. God knows what that kid was going through.

I could hear the usual percussion as I headed down the stairs to the gym. Without seeing anyone, I could tell from the sounds —like a hi-hat on a drum set—that it was probably Malik on the speed bag. Whoever was hitting it knew what they were doing. There was also the thudding bass I could hear on the heavy bag, and that was undoubtedly Piggy. Pig had been coming to the gym as long as I had. He was fat, didn't move well, and swung his punches from so far away you could count to 10 before they landed.

But if you took one of his body shots, you'd never shit right again.

When I came through the door, I saw I was right. There were also eight kids ready for the workout. Lorenzo's murder was on the news, so they would all know. He was a bigger-than-life figure to them, and they'd need to process this. I don't know how, but they would need to.

"Yo," I yelled. "Let's gather around. Take a seat on the floor. We got to talk a little."

Michael, Wali, Sheron, Jacob, Logan, Billy, Kareem, and Peter were there. Trevon wasn't.

"Everyone knows about Lorenzo. I think we gotta talk about it..." I said.

They all looked at each other. No one said a word.

"Why did they shoot him?" Kareem said. He was a mixed-race kid, with dark brown eyes and an unruly Afro. "Did he do something?"

"No." I shook my head. I didn't want to say they thought they were shooting at me.

"So, they just killed him for no reason? Like it was rando?" Wali said. He shook his head like he was trying to figure it out.

I felt a tension in my gut. The tension was guilt.

Lorenzo was dead because of me. But I couldn't tell them that.

"Will they catch who did it?" Peter asked.

Before I could say anything, Billy interrupted.

"They ain't gonna catch 'em. Cops never catch anyone in the 'hood."

I wasn't going to argue that point.

"Lorenzo was a good guy. He shouldn't have died," Sheron said.

Sometimes you need a 12-year-old to have things make sense.

That was when Trevon came in. He was moving slowly, and he had his head down with his red Yankees cap covering up his eyes. His shoulders were slumped, and it looked like he was trying to turn into himself.

"What's up, Tre?" I said and moved over to him. He turned

away. At 125 lbs, he was still a skinny kid, even if he had really good boxing skills for his age. "Hey man, come over here."

He turned slowly and lifted his head up.

His right eye was swollen shut. His lips were swollen, and his whole face was bruised. He stood in front of me so I could see.

It revolted me. It hit me in the gut with intensity that was part sadness and another whole part of something else.

Anger didn't describe it well enough.

"Who did this to you?" I said through my teeth.

## 26

"My father."

I looked at him for a long time. He had stifled his tears and was now showing more anger and feigned indifference.

"Your father? I thought, I thought you didn't have a father." It was a stupid thing to say.

"He's a piece of shit." Trevon looked away from me. "He said I had to learn that he was my father, not some nigger fighter. He said he would teach me until I learned."

I looked at Trevon. There were cigarette burns on his forearms.

My vision narrowed, and I could feel my heart beat.

"It won't happen again," I said.

Trevon looked at me and pursed his lips. He didn't say anything, but he was letting me know he didn't believe me.

"Where is he?"

Trevon shrugged. "He's usually on his corner. Clinton and Northern. He'll be with his boys."

I knew the corner. It was the heart of Jefferson Hill and the center of where bad things happened. If his father was there, he was a bad man and a dangerous one.

"What are you gonna do, Duff, talk to him?"

"Yeah. That's what I'm gonna do. What's his name?"

Trevon looked away.

"What's his name?" I repeated with a little more force.

"Angel. He's the one with the three teardrop ink under his eye."

I looked around the gym. There were the kids, Piggy and Malik. It was a pretty slow night.

I looked at Trevon.

"You lead the class." Then I yelled to Pig. "Yo P, you mind locking up?"

Piggy nodded.

I headed out to Clinton and Northern. It wasn't a long drive. It was already dark, and business would be picking up on the hill. If Angel was a dealer, then this was his prime work hour. I parked up Clinton and walked down the hill to the corner.

Thirty feet away, I saw a trio of men at the corner. At times like this, I didn't think. I just acted. The vision of Trevon's face, the cigarette burns, and his grief over Lorenzo flashed inside my head. The kid never had a break, and then he found a place for himself only to have it taken away, and his hell was returned. I didn't know if I could make things right for his life, but I knew what I could do.

I kept walking down to the corner.

"My man, you looking for some product?" The guy in the center spoke to me. I looked up and right into his face. He had the tears.

"You Trevon's father?" I said it flat and cold.

"Shit…what are you, social service?" He laughed, and his two boys joined in.

I hit him with a straight hard jab in the center of the face, and I heard and felt his nose crack. I pivoted and cracked the guy to his left with a backfist and spun around, catching the other guy in the temple with the side of my other fist. They both went down.

Angel had his hands over his nose. There was a lot of blood spilling through his fingers. I threw three left-hand crosses back into his nose, and he screamed and went down. One of the others jumped on my back, and I swung the crown of my head as hard as I could into his forehead and flipped him hard on his back onto the sidewalk. I heard the air rush out of him as he groaned and grabbed for his forehead.

The other rushed me with a looping right hand that came all the way from his side. I stepped inside it and hit him with a jab-cross that put him down. I turned and jumped with my knee on Angel's chest. I heard his sternum break, and he screamed. Then I hit him with a series of piston punches to his face until it was a bloody pulp with no discernible features.

Then the sirens came.

I stepped off of Angel.

The other two limped away.

Angel lay on the sidewalk. Blood formed a puddle around him.

He wasn't moving.

My chest was heaving. I just stared down at the body in front of me. It was all I could see. I didn't feel anything.

"Hands up! Hands up! Jerry, call a bus! Hands up!"

The voices were distant, and they didn't register.

**27**

———————

They tackled me to the sidewalk even though I didn't resist. They cuffed me behind my back; I banged my head on the cement, and I felt my face scrape against the gravel. Red lights flashed and reflected off the dilapidated buildings of the Hill. Next, they pulled me to my feet and stuffed me into the back of the squad car.

I saw EMTs lift the gurney and load it into the ambulance. The sheet covered the entire body, including the head, and my mind was beginning to sort things out.

In my rage, I beat a man to death with my hands.

I threw up down my chest, and with my hands cuffed, there was nothing I could do to intercept it.

"Throw up on your shirt, not the upholstery, asshole. We have to drive in this thing."

I threw up again and aimed the best I could into my lap. Some got on the seat and the floor.

"Oh, c'mon, asshole," the cop said.

I was brought to the North Station. I was booked and allowed a phone call. I called Fowler, the attorney, because he was the only lawyer I knew. They put me in a holding cell with three other guys. They were all Black. Two of them were really drunk and were lying on the cement floor asleep. The other guy sat on the bench.

"You're facing murder," he said to me. There was a hint of admiration in his tone. "Who'd you ice?"

I just looked at him and kept my mouth shut. On *Law and Order*, that was always the best move.

The rage had left me, and in its place was an overwhelming sense of anxiety and guilt. My thoughts raced, and I wanted to drink so bad. I threw up again on the floor.

"Damn, that shit gonna get nasty," my roommate said.

I killed a man, and it wasn't the first time. It was what was making me sick. The man deserved it, and I needed to protect Trevon, but like the other times, I was judge and jury, and, actually, I was playing God. I swore I wouldn't do it again. I swore it every time the nightmares came or on the days the intrusive thoughts and images came.

I saw the biker who forced young girls into whoring. He was wedged in a door frame while I pummeled him to death. There was the sociopath who was setting up Carl. He had a throwing star in his throat while I beat him. There was the cult leader I blew up with explosives and let burn. There was the Russian contender who was about to rape an innocent Mexican girl.

In my vision, they were all in a pile. The pile filled with blood covered them. The blood filled up the room, and I felt myself drowning. I tried to scream, but nothing came out.

Then, it went black.

"He's coming to," a detached voice said. "He's coming to."

I tried to speak. I tried to ask where I was.

"He's saying something," a different voice said.

My eyes blurred and went in and out of focus. I made out the hospital bed, the beeping monitor, the wires connecting me to it. I went to move my hands, but I was handcuffed to the bed rail.

"He's moving," a voice said.

A cop in uniform appeared and looked over the bed.

"Take it easy…" came out of his mouth. "Take it easy…"

"Where am I?" I said.

"He's coming around. What did he say?"

"He asked where he is," the cop answered.

"You're in Crawford Medical Center. You've been given drugs to calm you. You were very agitated. Be still the best you can."

I looked at the blurry figures. A male nurse, a female nurse, another guy in white, and a cop. I was in some deep shit. I didn't know a lot of what was going on, but I knew I was in some deep shit.

"We're going to give you something to sleep," the female was talking.

"No, I don't want it," I forced myself to annunciate.

The nurse was preparing a syringe.

"No!" I shouted. It came out clear this time.

She nodded at the other two, and I felt them put their hands on my chest to restrain me.

"No!" I screamed.

I felt the pinch in my upper left arm.

I screamed.

Then things went black.

**28**

_________

Fowler went on about how his hands were tied and that I didn't have much to hope for. He outlined a mental health defense and something about blind rage as a defense that probably wouldn't work.

Kelley appeared in the doorway.

"Officer, you can take a break," he said to the uniformed cop who was drowsing in the vinyl chair in the corner.

"Thanks, Detective," he said. He got up, ran a hand over his wrinkled shirt, grabbed his hat, and made his way out.

Kelley nodded at someone I couldn't see in the hallway. Kelley walked in. He had a very serious look on his face. Of course, he wouldn't be happy with me, but I had been through that before, and he really had good reason to be.

Behind him were three guys in suits and a woman with short hair in a beige business suit. The first two I recognized after a moment. It was Nogales and Woods, the two FBI guys who rousted me the night I went to see Kathy. The third guy was an older Italian guy. He was tall and thin with a prominent nose and smartly styled graying hair. I didn't recognize the woman.

"You know agents Nogales and Woods, right?" Kelley was all business. "This is Val Brewer." He nodded toward the female agent.

I nodded.

"My name is Cusano. Joseph Cusano," the third man said. He wasn't cheery. "I am, uh, affiliated with these agents, but you don't need to know how or why. Please don't ask."

I nodded. I was medicated, but even if I wasn't, I'm not sure I would've understood what the hell was going on.

"You, probably by accident, have stumbled into a very large international investigation. It is something the United States, Canada, and some other countries have been working on for years." He didn't smile. He just looked at me hard and steady.

He went on.

"We know you've been looking for Kathy Sullivan. She is incidental to our investigation, but she's important. As a very successful sex worker, she got involved in something over her head. She went into hiding, and that's where you came in."

I nodded. It was all I could do.

"You were hired to find her because her agent was losing money. That was small-time, even if to them it was a financial source of income. There's a much bigger issue at play here."

He paused. I don't know if it was for effect, but it didn't heighten the drama.

"Kathy Sullivan was forging her own way. She was building a competition to Mindfun. She was building her own sex work and pornography corporation in a model that set up the workers and performers as co-owners. They would be protected, have employee benefits, and would make a substantial amount of money. It is a completely different model than exists now in this industry, which often runs on free labor, intimidation, and, frankly, troubled and insecure women with, uh, issues."

I continued to nod. I wasn't even sure if this had to do with the effects of the medication.

"I think it has become obvious that she became a threat. If she successfully built her corporation, and the signs were that she was quite capable of it, Mindfun, and maybe more importantly, those who make their money from supplying them would be threatened. That's where the murders in Crawford come from. They were letting her know what was going to happen to her if they could find her. Like many of her other strategies, so far she's been able to outwit them."

He paused again. He took out a pack of cigarettes, packed it down, and lit one. Apparently, he wasn't concerned about being in a hospital.

"You've been arrested for murder. There were a bunch of witnesses, and even the worst assistant DAs in the world will make it stick. Certainly, that stumblebum Fowler isn't going to get you off."

"Stumblebum?" I said. Cusano ignored it.

"We know the guy you beat to death is a piece of shit that the world will be better without."

I started to feel sick and swallowed it back.

"There's an underworld figure, a high-ranking organized crime member, who heads up most of the illegal porn, human trafficking, and ugly smut stuff. We're talking the non-consensual, rape, and child pornography. It involves human trafficking from countries across the globe. We'd like to set you up to deal with him."

I nodded.

"If you get made, they'll kill you. If you pull off what we want, this murder charge goes away."

I nodded. I looked at Kelley. His face was blank, but he gave me an almost subliminal tipping of the head.

"I'm in," I said.

**29**

———

"The target's name is Nico Mastriani. Gambino family. Second generation. His old man was made, and he grew up in the life." Cusano took a drag from his cigarette, blowing the smoke out slowly. "Twenty-two years ago, he moved the family into human trafficking and online porn. Early adopter. A visionary, if you believe in that kind of thing."

"Yeah, real forward-thinker," I muttered.

"In the last five years, his operation has gotten worse—Mexican women promised citizenship, only to be trafficked and broken. Rape, torture, group stuff—sick shit." Cusano exhaled smoke. "Sells it to a select market. Private site. Quadruple security protocols. Weekly login changes. Virtually untraceable."

Charming. Just the kind of scum I wanted to get tangled with.

"And Kathy Sullivan?" I asked.

"She's a threat. Her co-op model would cut into Mindfun's share of the market. If she makes her site successful, more consumers will go to her for content. But more than that—she wouldn't touch Mastriani's niche. If she gains traction, fewer people are paying for his twisted garbage."

"And they killed four women just to send a message?"

"The message was for Kathy: Quit or die." Cusano flicked his cigarette butt into an ashtray. "They couldn't find her, so they made an example of her inventory."

Inventory. He said it like they were nothing but products on a shelf.

"What's the play here? You take Mastriani down, another scumbag takes his place," I said.

"Not our problem," Cusano said. "We're not the morality police. We don't give a shit about porn. But we can't let this level of depravity go unchecked."

"And the women?" I asked. "The ones you're using to bait him."

Cusano looked at me like I was speaking another language.

"What do you mean?"

"What happens to them after?"

"They're released and the charges are dropped."

"What charges?"

"Illegal entry."

"And then?"

Cusano took a deep breath, exhaled through his nose. "They get sent back."

"Deported."

"Yeah, I guess. That's the most likely outcome."

I nodded and let that roll around in my head. I didn't like it. Then I looked him dead in the eye.

"They stay," I said.

"What?" Cusano's face darkened.

"They stay," I repeated. "You get them visas, asylum,

whatever the hell you gotta do. If I do this for you, they get to reunite with their kids and live a life that doesn't involve getting sold. That's the deal."

Cusano's expression flattened. "You're not in a position to negotiate."

I leaned in, voice low.

"Cusano, you wouldn't be here if you weren't desperate. You need me more than I need you. I just buried my best friend, and I'm facing murder charges. I don't give a shit about my own skin. But I'll be damned if I help you sell these women out. So that's the price of admission, pal. Take it or leave it."

Cusano stared at me, jaw clenched so tight I thought he might crack a molar.

"You're insane," he said finally.

"Trust me. I know it better than anyone."

**30**

———

Cusano had me pick them up at the Motel 6 on Watervliet Boulevard in Albany. It was an hour and a half ride to the city, and though it wasn't in the heart of the ghetto, it had the feel of being just on the outskirts. US 90 practically emptied into the parking lot, and from the other direction, it was a straight shot right to Arbor Hill, which was the place in the capital city that you didn't want to be in.

I didn't have names. Instead, I was told they'd be out front and they'd be easy to recognize. Cusano said there'd be three Mexican women in their early twenties or late teens, and they'd be made up and attractive. I wasn't sure what that meant, but I figured Cusano knew what he was doing.

I saw them right away. They were in tight jeans, high heels, and each had a lot of makeup. What I hadn't counted on was for there to be four little children and two men. The tallest of the women, a slender woman with skin the color of creamed coffee, must've recognized my car and hurriedly, in a panic, ushered the kids and the two men into their hotel room.

The second woman was curvier and perhaps a little

overweight, though it didn't stop her from wearing ridiculously tight acid-washed jeans and a red halter. Her press-on nails had glitter on the tips, and her lips were somehow outlined in matching glitter. The third woman looked like she was barely sixteen, and maybe because of her age, the tight jeans made almost completely of Lycra and the matching skin-tight top seemed even more obscene. She had very light skin like an Anglo and very thin lips.

"I'm Duffy," I said. I don't know what I was thinking. These women thought I was getting ready to sell them into a life of prostitution. It was hard to believe they would want to be buddies. "What are your names?"

They looked at each other and then back at me.

"Como se llama?" It was probably all I had left from high school Spanish.

They spoke in order, "Maria," "Sucre," and "Susanna." None of them made eye contact.

The sight of the kids and what I imagined were husbands resonated with me. It made them that much more flesh and blood. I felt it in my body, and it didn't feel good.

From there, I was to head back onto 90, get off at Wolf Road, and in a mile I would pull into the Marriott where Mastriani's men would meet me. Once there, money would be exchanged, and the FBI, or whoever the hell I was working for, would have him on trafficking and the women would be released.

I saw no signs of law enforcement—local police, FBI, or a SWAT—anywhere near the Marriott. I pulled in and, as instructed, parked in the far end of the lot closest to the road. I put the car in park and brought the ladies out of the back seat. I held the door as they got out, and the smell of heavy cheap perfume almost made me gag. Each of them struggled getting out of the back seat with their high heels, making their first few steps awkward.

A Mercedes SUV pulled up, and a dark-haired weightlifting type with a black leather jacket, black silk shirt, and gold chain got out.

"Duffy, right?" he said without introducing himself or even acknowledging the three women. "Follow me."

I nodded to the women, and we headed inside the Marriott. It was your typical high-end chain hotel with an amazingly clean lobby, a small bar off of it with just a few patrons, and soft piano music playing over the speaker system.

Black leather jacket walked past the front desk and went right to the elevator. We followed in behind and hit the button for the 11th floor, which said, "Gold Member Suites." He took off his sunglasses and looked at the women like he was a thoroughbred auction.

"They'll do fine." He said it without smiling.

## 31

The *ping* of the elevator felt like a countdown clock ticking toward something bad. I adjusted my collar, trying to ignore the itch at the back of my neck. They had me wired up, and it was the only thing I could feel. It itched, and it reminded me of what I was about to do and the chances of it not working out well for me.

The suite at the Marriot was on the top floor and made to look exclusive. There were floor-to-ceiling windows with a view of the city lights. Plush carpet, leather couches, a bar stocked with overpriced bourbon, and all the trappings that went with whatever membership Mastriani had. It smelled of men's cologne and high-end hotel room deodorizer.

Mastriani stood near the glass table in the center of the room. His shiny gray suit was pressed, and he had a starched white shirt open at the collar and a red polka-dotted pocket square. His big gold watch and gold chain completed the look. It was the look that scumbag wise guys thought was classy. The three women stood near the king-sized bed, their backs pressed to the wall. They were doing their best to not look terrified. They failed.

Nico looked me in the eye like he was trying to let me know he was evaluating me. He swirled the amber liquid in his glass and sipped it in that affected way guys trying to make an impression did.

"You know, I appreciate you arranging this meeting, Dombrowski. You and I? We're business partners now."

I forced a grin. "Yeah, partners. I guess you could say that."

I could feel the wire against my skin, and I thought of the FBI listening in from their van parked somewhere on the street. This was supposed to be simple—just a human trafficking sting. The feds wanted Nico saying the right words on tape, and I was supposed to be the guy who made sure he did.

But then he turned to the women.

"Before we get to the paperwork," Carmine said, setting his drink down, "I think I'm gonna get better acquainted with the merchandise. It is important to the process."

I didn't like the sound of this.

Carmine loosened his tie and rolled up his sleeves. He looked at the women from top to bottom like they were meat. There was no acknowledgment of their humanity. One of the women flinched. Another swallowed hard and stared at the floor.

I started to get that feeling. It was a sick feeling, and I hated it. It was the feeling I had to exorcise. It was the feeling that brought me to Trevon's father.

I heard the click of a belt buckle.

*That's it.*

"No, that's not happening, Nico," I said. It was loud, flat, and determined.

He was running his hands through two of the women's hair while looking at the other.

"Not your business, kid." He said it without looking at me. He reached down to grope the first woman's breast.

I grabbed him by the collar of his suit, ripping the seam, and spun him around into the wall. He hit it hard.

"What the fuck—" He gasped, but he didn't get to finish. I hit him with a left-right-left series of body shots, and he crumpled to the ground.

The muscle guy lurched forward and, like they always do, swung a hard but wide hook at my head. My adrenaline was through the roof, but I still loved it. I stepped slightly to my right, pivoted, threw a right jab that landed flush on his nose, and turned my hips to deliver a left cross that landed on the point of his chin. He was out before he face-planted in the carpet.

"Duffy!" My earpiece crackled, some fed yelling in my ear. "Stand down! We're moving in!"

Screw that.

Mastriani was back up. He was wobbly, and he reached for the back of his slacks. I didn't hesitate. I skipped forward and threw a snap kick into his solar plexus and followed that with an elbow to his temple. He went down, landing hard on his side when he crashed. The butt of the gun was still in the small of his back. I reached down, pulled it out, and pointed it at his face.

Mastriani coughed, spit blood onto the carpet, then looked up at me with a mouthful of red. "You just screwed yourself, Dombrowski."

I knelt down, moved my gun to my left hand, and used my right. I grabbed him by the throat and squeezed just enough to make the point. "Yeah? You were about to rape three women. You think I give a damn about screwing myself?"

The suite door crashed open. A flood of FBI agents swarmed in, guns drawn. The lead guy wore a windbreaker, work pants, and tactical boots. He had an earpiece. He did all the talking.

"Hands up!"

I stepped back, my chest heaving, trying to catch my breath. There were two bodies on the floor, only one conscious.

"FBI! Hands up, Mastriani!"

"Duffy, what the fuck's your problem! You *promised* you wouldn't interfere! This is totally fucked."

I just looked at him.

"Asshole! You might've just fucked the whole case. The money was never exchanged. You fucked it all!"

I looked past him at the three women. One of them met my eyes—just for a second. I could see what was behind them. There was plenty of fear still there, but there was also a hint of relief. There might have been a hint of gratitude.

I looked at him.

"Yeah?" I said, my voice low. "I can live with that."

The agent glared, then turned away, barking orders to his team. Mastriani was cuffed and escorted through the door while the women were hurried out of the room.

I knew I'd just bought myself a world of trouble. The feds would rip me apart for this, and Mastriani's people would want their own kind of payback.

But as I watched the elevator doors close on those women, I knew one thing.

Some lines you just don't let people cross.

**32**

I was in a squad room in a non-descript federal building. I had driven past the building my whole life and didn't realize what it was. There were no signs in front or anything. It was a one-story brick building that looked like it might be part of a school, except it wasn't.

The room's fluorescent lights buzzed, and their harsh glow made Cusano and the others that much more stark and menacing. The door opened, and a guy I didn't recognize came in.

"I am assistant federal prosecutor Mark Downes." He let his portfolio drop on the metal table in front of me. It made a loud thud. "Do you have any idea what you've done, Dombrowski?" he snapped, tossing a folder onto the table. "You compromised a federal operation!"

He stared at me the way people in authority do when they think they're badasses by virtue of their title. Things went differently in a boxing gym. I stared right back.

"I'd do it again," I said.

Downes sighed and rubbed his temples.

"This isn't about your charming fucking view of justice. This is about protocol. This is about the law. This is about a three-year investigation into organized crime that you just fucked up."

"Look, whatever the fuck your name is, I'm sorry I screwed your chance to get an adult gold star on your spelling test. I stopped a fuckin' pig from raping three innocent women who you set up to be pawns in this bullshit. Fuck you, asshole. I'd do it again. I'd do it a thousand times."

I was shouting by the end of my last sentence.

He just looked at me.

"The federal attorney had a deal with you to make your murder charges go away. I'm recommending that be taken off the table. See how righteous you'll feel doing 25 to life." He picked up his portfolio and stormed out the door.

Cusano stood up.

"Duffy, he's serious. I get what you did, but there was no money exchanged. There was no crime. Now we got nothing." He lit a cigarette and exhaled hard. "I wouldn't worry too much about murder charges. You beat up Nico Mastrianni in front of one of his men, no less. You're as good as dead already. Watch your back."

I didn't say anything to that.

Cusano was right. I was fucked. I'd been in trouble before, brought on by my heroics, but never quite like this.

They said I could go, and I have to admit, it dawned on me that freedom was going to be nice, but not with this new bull's-eye on my back. It was a good three miles back to the Marriott where I left my car, and twice that to the bar. After getting the car I decided to head to the bar. No sense returning to the scene of the crime, so to speak.

Besides, I needed to think.

Kathy. That's what got me into all of this. Kathy's pursuit of a kindler and gentler profession for those who make their living helping guys get their rocks off. Three sex workers were dead. Carlton was dead. Lorenzo was dead. Zo might be dead because he was protecting women.

I walked past the ball fields and basketball courts of Second Avenue. The sun had gone down, and there was a chill in the air. I turned up Twiller Street to get off the main street.

Meanwhile, Kathy remained a ghost. Fine and dandy that she had great business acumen and was setting up a whoring conglomerate, but it didn't seem quite right that she was in some sort of safe madame ivory tower while chaos swirled below her.

It didn't seem right at all.

I crossed over Delaware Avenue and headed up Ten Eyk to Academy and past the Albany Academy.

I was halfway back to the bar when a dark sedan pulled up beside me. The window rolled down, and there she was—Brewer, the female agent from Cusano's crew. I'd seen her before in that dull briefing room, in the background, with nothing to say.

"Duffy," she said. "We found Kathy."

I froze.

"What?"

"This is a courtesy. You want in or not?"

"In, meaning what?" I asked. "Suddenly the feds are my best friends again?"

"Look, the bullshit that went down was the federal attorney, not us. We're on your side. Get in." She moved the car into drive but kept her foot on the brake. I got in. I'm not sure why.

"Where's Cusano?" I asked.

"He sent me. He would bring too much attention to this." She kept driving with her eyes straight ahead.

"Where is she?" I asked what was probably the most obvious question.

"She's holed up in a warehouse off Vatrano Dr. She had a friend lend her an office in the warehouse district."

I nodded, but something didn't feel right.

Trevon, Lorenzo, Carlton, and the others. I felt like I had to act. I'd sort it all later.

"How'd you find her?" I said.

"She made contact," the agent said, eyes on the road. "She wants out."

"Out? I thought she was doing her own thing. Starting her own conglomerate."

"Uh, out in that she needs to come out of hiding and get some protection."

I turned that around in my head.

"Why do you need me?"

"Courtesy, and you know the players now. You can be a comfort to her."

"I haven't seen her in a decade."

She didn't answer. She ran a red light and swerved around someone who had the nerve to be going 30 in a 30.

I stared out the window. Maybe this was the break. Or maybe it was just another round of the universe seeing how much it could pile on.

We pulled down Vatrano. It was a series of warehouses, converted gyms, and buildings to store products and equipment. We took it all the way down to the end, about half a mile.

"Really? Here?" I said.

"Well, who would think of looking here?"

She had a point.

The sign over the door said "Wilson Barber and Beauty Supply."

She got out, walked to the door, flashed a key fob, and opened the door.

I followed.

Inside was a long corridor with a series of doors numbered from 1 to 8. I followed her down to the end of the corridor to an unnumbered door.

She flashed the fob again. The door clicked open.

"She's inside," she said. Then she stepped aside.

I took two steps in and froze.

Mastrianni.

## 33

The room was a converted warehouse space made to look like a lounge. A meeting table off to the side with office chairs, several living room chairs, a couch, and a wet bar in the corner. It reminded me of the room in The Sopranos in the back of the bar. Mastrianni was sipping his scotch from a heavy ornate rocks glass.

Kathy was tied to a chair and gagged, naked and shaking, eyes wide with terror.

The room swarmed with guns. Four or five men, maybe more. Their barrels all pointed one way.

"Dombrowski," Mastrianni said, like he was inviting me to Thanksgiving dinner. "Thanks for coming." He laughed.

I turned to look at the agent. She closed the door softly and leaned against it.

"Sorry, Duffy," she said. "Just business."

Mastrianni raised his glass. "Time for the final act."

My throat went dry, my heart raced, and I couldn't think. I knew I was screwed.

A couple of Mastrianni's goons grabbed me. They dragged

me into the room and threw me against the wall, and my head bounced off the cinder block. I slumped to the floor.

Mastrianni stood over Kathy, sleeves rolled up, straight out of the mobster dress code. His swollen, broken face from our last meeting didn't make him any prettier.

"You ruined a good thing, Dombrowski," he said, adjusting the knot on his tie like he was about to sit down for a steak. "You could've walked away after the deal. You could've kept your mouth shut. But no, you had to play hero."

I always loved how real-life mobsters based their banter on the movies they've seen.

"You cost me product, you cost me money, and you embarrassed me." He stopped and looked down at Kathy, stroking her chin with two fingers. "Now you get to watch."

Kathy's eyes were wild, furious, terrified.

Mastrianni snapped his fingers. A goon stepped forward with a knife.

"We'll keep it slow," Mastrianni said, smiling.

The knife pressed against Kathy's thigh. She flinched, tried to pull away, but the ropes held. The blade broke skin, and a thin line of blood slid down her leg. Her muffled scream made something inside of me go bad.

I lunged, but two heavies had me by the arms. I couldn't move. My throat tightened. I could barely breathe.

"Look at him, boys," Mastrianni said. "That's what heartbreak looks like."

That's when the door exploded.

Literally.

The wood splintered, and the sound was deafening. Men poured in, masks, black tactical suits, automatic rifles, and the total look of professionals.

Mastrianni's grin disappeared. Guns went up. Kathy ducked her head. I hit the floor.

And then all hell broke loose.

The gunfire exploded in the room. Muzzle flashes lit up the room like a Fourth of July explosion. I dove behind a leather couch as the walls splintered and glass rained down from the shattered windows. Screams echoed off the high-rise walls—panic, orders barked from the goons, and the cold methodical commands from whoever had crashed the party.

I crawled on my elbows across the ruined carpet, trying to keep low. A round tore through the couch, inches from my head. Another snapped past my ear. I rolled behind a tipped-over table and came up just enough to see Kathy. She was still tied to the chair, screaming behind the gag, eyes darting between the chaos and me.

I needed to get to her.

A goon spotted me and raised his pistol. Instinct took over. It was all I had. I launched the table at him, closed the distance, and threw a right hook that would've made Smitty proud. The guy dropped like a sack of potatoes.

The noise didn't stop. The place sounded like a war zone.

I turned and saw Mastrianni slipping toward the back door, dragging Kathy with him, one hand gripping her arm, the other holding a snub-nosed revolver.

I chased them, vaulting over busted furniture and ducking wild shots. We ended up in a smaller room, just off the other. Kathy was thrown to the floor. Mastrianni spun, gun pointed straight at me.

"End of the line, Dombrowski," he sneered. His lip curled over his cracked teeth, blood still dried from our last encounter. "You got no badge, no backup, and no deal."

I froze. He cocked the hammer back, eyes gleaming like he'd been waiting for this.

"You think you've been playing the hero? All you've done is screw up everything. Now you get to die knowing it didn't mean a damn thing."

Then came the sound I'll never forget.

A sharp crack.

Mastrianni staggered forward. Behind him, Trevon stood holding an aluminum baseball bat like he was back at the gym, channeling every bit of Lorenzo's lessons. The kid's eyes were locked in—not scared, not angry—just deadly calm.

Mastrianni's gun skittered across the floor.

I moved to grab it, but Trevon stepped between us.

"Let me," he said.

Before I could stop him, he went to work. Fast, sharp shots, short punches just like Lorenzo taught him. Trevon wasn't wild or sloppy; he was surgical, like he knew exactly where to hit and how hard. Mastrianni couldn't answer back, couldn't even stand against the flurry.

I stood frozen for a moment, watching the kid fight like a pro.

Then I saw it—the rage, the risk of going too far. Trevon had reached for the bat, raised it high, and was ready to deliver the final blow.

"Trevon!" I shouted.

His chest heaved. His grip tightened.

"Trevon, don't," I said, softer this time. "You don't want to carry this."

His eyes locked on mine. His chest heaved; he didn't blink. He just looked at Mastrianni, splayed on the floor, his face a bloody mess. He writhed in pain.

"He killed Lorenzo. He should die," Trevon said.

I continued to hold him.

"No," I said. "Not like this. Not now."

We stood silently. I didn't let go for a long time. Tre started to cry. It was soft, and then the intensity increased. Slowly, the bat lowered. He stepped back, sank to the floor, and wept.

Mastrianni was out cold but breathing.

The room was wrecked. Kathy sobbed on the floor. Trevon stood, wiped his eyes with his sleeves, and sniffed. He looked at Mastrianni and then at me.

"The Caretaker let me come. I was supposed to stay in the parking lot," Trevon said.

"The Caretaker, you know him?" I said.

"Lorenzo did." Trevon looked at me. "He was helping The Caretaker."

## 34

---

The room filled up with cops of all shapes, sizes, and jurisdictions. You could hear sirens in the distance, staticky radio speakers, and the persistent murmur of discussions. The firefight was over, but the room was still energized—like there was a current of electricity running through it.

I was leaning against a wall, not even trying to stop my chest from heaving or getting my body to settle. Kathy, wrapped in a gray blanket by one of the responding EMTs, sat on the edge of a couch, silent. Her face was bloodied, but her eyes were sharp, focused, and alive. She was breathing, which was more than I could've hoped for ten minutes ago.

Outside the door to the room, the hallway was a swarm of uniforms. Cops and tactical units rushed in waves—some clearing rooms, some corralling handcuffed survivors. EMTs navigated the mess, triaging bodies, calling for stretchers, trying to make sense of what the hell had just gone down.

I felt a hand on my shoulder. I turned. It was Kelley, already looking tired, already sweating through his shirt.

"You okay?" Kelley asked. The guy endlessly gave me shit for the stuff I got involved in and would doubtless do it for this situation. Not now, though; now he was a friend.

"Uh, not sure. Probably not," I said. "But I'm not dead. That's something."

Kelley nodded. "What the hell happened?"

I let my head fall back against the wall, then looked across the room. "They were going to kill her. They had me dead to rights. Somebody—someone—came through that door and started shooting."

Kelley followed my gaze to the blood trail near the entryway, EMTs clustered around a body on the floor, one of them barking vitals into a radio.

"That guy..." Kelley said slowly, walking forward, ducking under a strip of hanging drywall to get a better look. "Jesus. I know him."

"Yeah?" I said.

Kelley crouched next to the EMT, motioning for a peek. His face went cold. "It's The Caretaker."

"You sure?" I couldn't believe what I was hearing.

Kelley nodded. "You don't work in law enforcement around here and not know him."

"He saved me. He saved Kathy. He and Trevon."

"He's barely alive," Kelley said, his voice low. "Multiple gunshot wounds. Chest. Leg. Possibly gut."

An EMT shouted for a stretcher. They moved quickly, strapping The Caretaker down, working intubation and IV lines in fluid tandem.

"Is he gonna make it?" Duffy asked.

Kelley shrugged. "They're saying critical. If he makes it, it won't be pretty."

I felt that settle in my chest. The man who moved in shadows, who brokered blood with cold detachment, had walked into a slaughterhouse—for them.

"What the hell was he doing here?" Kelley asked.

I looked at Kathy, who still hadn't spoken, and then at Trevon, who stood in the doorway still holding on to his bat, his eyes wide but unblinking.

"I think it had something to do with standing up for something. He didn't like what was going on," I said.

"Somebody was threatening his business?" Kelley asked.

"I think it was something more than that. I think he and Lorenzo didn't like the ugly shit."

Kelley didn't answer. He seemed to mull that over while he kept working. He kept staring at the stretcher as it disappeared down the hallway.

I turned back into the room. Kathy was still sitting on the couch, shoulders hunched beneath the scratchy gray blanket, blood still dried on her lip. She looked small, almost delicate, but her eyes held steady when she spotted him.

I scanned the room. Brewer was cuffed and with a uniformed cop. Something told me she was found out. Clearly working both sides and it blew up in her face.

Kathy spoke to me.

"Duffy?" she said, her voice rough but sure.

"Yeah." He stepped closer, not knowing what else to say.

Kathy gave the faintest of smirks, tired and bitter all at once. She raised her hand, miming a toast with an invisible glass.

"Well," she said. "Here's to old times."

Duffy felt a chill crawl up his neck. He wasn't sure if it was the night's violence or the way she said it. Maybe both.

He gave her a nod. "Yeah. Here's to old times."

And neither of us smiled.

## 35

I t was a long night with lots of different cops. Cops of all shapes and sizes, rank, uniforms, and attitudes. They took The Caretaker to the hospital, and all I knew was he was in bad shape. He wasn't exactly a friend, and heroics probably had more to do with his business interests than it did with his loyalty to me. Still, he saved my life, and his motivation didn't matter.

The Caretaker getting shot also meant I wouldn't be getting paid, or at least I wouldn't be getting paid in the near future, which meant there was no hope for the bar. That stabbed me in the gut when I thought about it, but after the last 24 hours, it was tough to get worked up about anything that wasn't life or death.

And Mastrianni? Well, they arrested him, and he was charged with everything from attempted murder to kidnapping to human trafficking. That probably meant Kathy was safe, at least for the time being. Did it mean poor women weren't going to be exploited and used in porn and prostitution?

Not a chance.

I didn't delude myself into thinking anything else.

I did find Kathy. I did get three women asylum.

Kathy was free to do all sorts of MBAish stuff and create the most profitable, sex work-positive, healthiest, women-first sex business the world has ever seen. She could get rich, women would be safer and richer, and have a great HMO and employee benefit plan.

Somehow, it all didn't warm my heart.

Right now, though, I needed to sleep. After I slid Al across the comforter and my head hit the pillow, I was out. I mean really out. Death's cousin, a sound exhausted type of sleep. There was nothing peaceful about it, but it was heavy and deep.

The sharp knock at the first-floor door yanked me out of it. Three hard raps, urgent and official. Al lifted his head from the foot of the bed and gave a half groan, half sigh, like he was too tired to even bark. I rubbed my eyes and shuffled down the stairs to the door, and when I opened it, two men stood there. Police uniforms but not Crawford police.

"Mr. Dombrowski," the taller one said. "I'm Officer Fernandes, this is Officer Murphy. We are with the U.S. Marshals. We need you to come with us."

I squinted at them. "What the hell for?"

The shorter one, Murphy, stepped forward and pulled out a folded document. "You're under arrest for the murder of Angel Santiago."

I didn't believe what I heard. "There was a deal in place."

Neither one of them looked like they had much of a sense of humor.

"You've got to be kidding," I said again, louder this time. "We had a deal. Cusano, the whole bunch of you—there was a deal."

"You can take that up with the U.S. Attorney," Fernandes said, already reaching for the cuffs.

I backed up a step, still trying to wake up, still trying to process it.

"No, no, no. This isn't right. I put myself in the middle of your mess. You all needed me. The sting, the set-up, all of it. And now you're coming here with cuffs? After everything?"

Al had joined me downstairs, confused but ready. He barked once. He didn't like the two cops.

"You want to put on some clothes?" Murphy asked, like I was inconveniencing him.

I stood there in a T-shirt and sweatpants, trying to piece together how this could possibly be happening. But they weren't negotiating. They weren't apologizing. Just doing a job.

"Get your clothes. We'll give you a minute," Fernandes said.

I closed the door without saying anything, went to the bedroom, and stared at the closet like I might find a better option in there. But there wasn't one.

Five minutes later, they walked me out, cuffed like I was some thug they pulled off the corner. No fanfare. No explanations. Just another trip through the meat grinder.

And the worst part?

I wasn't even surprised.

## 36

The holding cell smelled like a combination of Lysol and desperation. Kelley stopped by the next morning, coffee in hand, and stood outside the bars like we were two old pals meeting for breakfast.

"You got mail," he said, holding up a folded piece of paper.

"That's dramatic," I said.

"It's from the bank." He passed it through the bars.

I unfolded it. It wasn't unexpected, but it still hit like a well-placed left hook. The bar's mortgage was being called in. The clock had run out, and with no backup funds, no Hail Mary, and no magic federal payout, I was done.

I let the paper drop onto the cold floor.

"So that's that," I said.

Kelley leaned against the bars. "I'm sorry, Duff. You put your heart into that place."

"Yeah, well, my heart's been wrong before."

He didn't argue.

The bar wasn't just a job. It wasn't just a place where drunk regulars swapped bad trivia and cried into their third

Narragansett. It was the only thing I had left tying me to anything that resembled community. Wild, weird, broken community.

"You gonna tell them yet?" Kelley asked.

I knew he meant Billy, the Recovery Group, the Foursome, all of them.

"Not yet."

He nodded. "You'll figure it out."

I wasn't so sure.

I had nothing left but an arraignment, a failing defense, and a basset hound waiting for me on the outside.

And still, somehow, it felt like I wasn't finished.

## 37

The courtroom was one of those ancient ones they show on the local news, all stained wood paneling and worn-out leather chairs. It smelled like mildew and disappointment. Fowler, bless his clueless soul, sat beside me with two open briefcases worth of paperwork, most of which looked like he picked it up from the discount pile at a garage sale.

Judge Killian presided. A no-nonsense, sharp-chinned woman who made you sit straighter just by walking into the room.

The ADA, a slick federal type who made sure to flash his badge holder every time he moved, stood at the ready. This was a formality for him. The charge was open and shut, especially after my little extracurricular at Clinton and Northern.

Fowler shuffled through his papers, wiping donut glaze off his tie as he did.

The first twenty minutes went just how I figured. The prosecutor laid out the facts like a well-rehearsed play. The judge scribbled notes, and Fowler sat there looking like he was watching a hockey game he didn't understand.

Then it happened.

Fowler reached for his coffee, knocking over half his file pile onto the floor. Papers scattered everywhere. As he stooped to gather them, he froze.

He stood there reading this sheet of paper and everything stopped.

"Your Honor," Fowler said, holding up a sheet of paper. "If I may, I think we have an issue."

The judge peered over her glasses. "Mr. Fowler, I assume you're not wasting my time."

"No, no," Fowler said, wiping his forehead. He held up the page like it was the Holy Grail. "There's no signed cooperation agreement. Not by Duffy, not by the U.S. Attorney's Office. Just a memo referencing it. The form was left blank and never signed."

"You're just finding this now? Thank God you spilled your coffee," The judge said not trying to restrain her sarcasm.

The prosecutor rolled his eyes. "Your Honor, we had a verbal agreement. The defendant was aware—"

"Counselor," Judge Killian cut him off. "Verbal agreements don't cut it in this courtroom, especially with murder on the line."

The prosecutor started to protest when, from the gallery, Agent Nogales casually handed a folded paper over the railing to the defense table.

Fowler, clueless as ever, unfolded it. His eyes got big.

"Uh, Your Honor, additionally—uh, here's an email from Special Agent Cusano explicitly promising that Mr. Dombrowski would not be prosecuted if he assisted the bureau." Fowler handed it to the clerk.

The judge read it. Twice.

The room went dead silent.

"It is remarkable how things keep landing in your lap counselor," The judge said.

The prosecutor's jaw tightened. Fowler handed the email print out to the judge.

"You're kidding me," the judge said, mostly to herself.

She slammed her gavel.

"Charges dismissed."

Fowler blinked.

I blinked.

I think even Fowler's coffee blinked.

"You're free to go, Mr. Dombrowski," Judge Killian said.

Just like that.

Outside the courtroom, I caught up to Nogales.

"Why?" I asked.

He didn't even slow down. "Call it a professional courtesy." Then he was gone.

I wasn't sure if I'd just been saved or set up for something worse.

Either way, I was out.

**38**

---

I walked to the bar in a daze. Not like I was floating, not like I was triumphant—more like a guy who'd survived a plane crash and wasn't sure what planet he was on. The morning air cut through my shirt, but I didn't bother zipping up my coat. I was free. And somehow, that didn't feel like enough.

When I got to the front door, I hesitated.

The bar was more than a business. It was a pulse. Mine, mostly. And now, that pulse was fading. There was no money. No plan. I'd fought for people. For Kathy. For Lorenzo. For Trevon. But no one was fighting for the place that held us all together.

I pushed open the door and got ready to say goodbye.

Instead, I heard music.

Laughter.

And cheering.

The place was packed.

Patti was sitting in her usual seat, wearing a plastic tiara. Rocco was doing his bad Elvis impression with a broom for a microphone. Pasquale was waving a Narragansett like he'd just won a prizefight.

Confetti rained down in slow, lazy clumps. Someone had dragged in balloons. Someone else made a cake. And in the middle of it all, Billy stood behind the bar with a goofy smile and two hands raised.

"You're back!" he yelled over the music.

"I'm… what the hell is going on?"

"We're celebrating!" Kim yelled. "You're not closing the bar!"

I blinked. "Uh… yes, I am."

Billy hopped over to the register like a man about to take a bow.

"Nope," he said. "We're all set."

He pulled out a piece of paper and handed it to me. A New York State Lottery claim form. Signed. Validated.

"Remember those scratch-offs the Recovery Group kept leaving on the bar? The ones you never checked?" Billy's eyes danced. "I checked 'em all."

My heart stopped.

"One of them hit?" I asked.

Billy grinned. "A hundred thousand bucks."

I nearly sat down on the floor.

"You're serious."

"Dead serious. I already talked to the lottery folks. Took it down this morning. The bar's safe, Duff. You're safe."

The Foursome burst into applause.

Ky gave a solemn nod. "Told you not to toss 'em."

I looked around the bar at all these mismatched pieces of my life: Patti, Kim, Pasquale, Rocco, and the Jerrys. Kelley offered a quiet salute from the end of the bar.

And the Recovery Group huddled near the dartboard with paper cups of coffee, smiling but not saying much.

"Who scratched the winning one?" I asked.

They all pointed at each other, arguing like kids who didn't want credit.

"Doesn't matter," Ky finally said. "Guess we were all meant to be part of it."

I looked at Billy.

"You sure it wasn't you?"

He shook his head. "It wasn't me."

I let out a long, slow breath and looked around.

"Alright," I said. "Drinks on the house."

They cheered again like it was New Year's Eve.

**39**

———

The next morning, the bar looked like it always did after a party—chairs askew, confetti clinging to the walls, the scent of stale beer, and the faint smell of burnt coffee. I was behind the bar with a mop when Billy came in, whistling like he didn't have a care in the world.

He leaned on the bar like he owned the place.

"Morning, Duff."

"Morning," I said, pushing the mop bucket aside. "You're early."

"Yeah, figured I'd help clean up after the salvation party," he said, smiling. Then he got this fidgety look like he was holding something back.

"You got something on your mind?" I asked.

He scratched the back of his neck. "Yeah. About last night. The lottery ticket."

"What about it?"

"It wasn't the ticket."

I stopped mopping. "What do you mean?"

Billy reached into his coat and pulled out an envelope. It was thick and sealed with red wax. He handed it to me.

"She came in right after you left for court," Billy said. "Blonde. Beautiful. Real calm about it."

I cracked the seal and found inside a cashier's check made out to me. One hundred thousand dollars. Alongside it, a simple folded piece of paper.

On it was written:

"This is love for me. — K"

I stared at it. The handwriting was perfect, almost like it had been practiced.

Billy kept talking, filling the silence.

"She told me not to tell you. Said you'd be stubborn about it if you knew. Wanted you to think the group saved the place."

I just stared at the note.

"She said it was between you and her. That's all she'd give me."

I slumped against the bar.

"Was it Kathy?" Billy asked, his voice soft.

I didn't answer.

I just folded the note, slid it back into the envelope, and tucked it in my coat pocket.

"It was someone who knows what love is," I said.

Billy frowned. "Didn't she say money was love to her?"

I thought about that. About the scene in the warehouse. About the way she looked at me as the cops led her out wrapped in a blanket. About the note.

"Maybe sometimes," I said. "Maybe sometimes it is."

Billy gave me a quiet nod and went back to scrubbing down the tables, leaving me alone with my thoughts and the echo of a woman who still managed to surprise me.

## 40

The bar felt different that night. It wasn't the decorations or the cleaned-up mess from the party. It wasn't the repaired neon sign humming a little steadier or even the old jukebox softly playing a Sinatra tune.

It was quiet.

Not the empty kind of quiet. The settled kind. The bar was still standing. The mortgage was paid for another year. The lights were still on. And somehow, so was I.

I sat in my usual stool at the end of the bar, nursing a coffee. No whiskey. Not tonight.

I thought about Lorenzo. About Trevon, who was back living with me for now. About Billy and the recovery group still treating the place like their second home. About the Caretaker, clinging to life somewhere. About Kathy. About everyone and everything that got me here.

It wasn't the first time I wondered what the hell I was doing with my life. I always circled back to the same answer — doing the best I could with what I had. Maybe that's all any of us do.

The front door creaked.

Trina.

She stepped in, looking like she just came from work. Slacks, blouse, soft blue scarf wrapped around her neck. Her eyes found me without hesitation, like they always did.

"Hey," she said.

"Hey." I motioned to the empty bar. "Place is all yours."

She gave me a small smile. "Good. Less competition."

I stood, walked around the bar, and we fell into each other's arms without a word.

After a long moment, she pulled back just enough to look at me.

"You okay?" she asked.

"No." I shook my head. "But I'm here."

She kissed me softly, like we had all the time in the world.

Without another word, I locked up, flipped the bar lights off, and we went upstairs.

Inside the apartment, I didn't put on the television. I didn't make small talk. I just held her.

And when we made love, it wasn't frantic or cinematic. It was quiet. Familiar. Tender. Human.

It was, I realized, the opposite of what all of this had been about — the deals, the trades, the cheap sales of bodies and lives.

This wasn't a transaction.

This was what the whole messed-up story had been fighting against.

After, we laid there, tangled up, listening to the city outside, breathing the same soft breath.

I thought about Kathy's note.

"This is love for me."

I closed my eyes.

Maybe she wasn't wrong.

Maybe neither was I.

And somewhere between the noise and the quiet, I figured that was enough.

# DUFFY'S FIGHT CLUB

Join "Duffy's Fight Club" for free short thrillers, an audio book, Tom's magazine work, a video on judging boxing, Tom's appearance on "Copy Cat Killers" and Rocky the blood hound singing "My Way."
TomSchreck.com.

# EPILOGUE

The next morning, I walked Al along the cracked sidewalks of Crawford. The city was waking up, half-asleep and already behind schedule. Al sniffed every lamppost like it was the first time.

I thought about Lorenzo and Trevon, about Kathy and The Caretaker, about the bar and the oddball family that somehow assembled itself there. I thought about Trina, still upstairs in bed, probably stealing all the covers.

I didn't know if any of it made sense. I just knew it mattered.

Al stopped at a hydrant, lifted his leg, and looked up at me like I should've known better.

"You and me both, buddy," I said.

And we kept walking.

The End

# ABOUT THE AUTHOR

Tom Schreck is the author of *The Duffy Series* and the stand alone thrillers *Getting Dunn* and *Redeeming Trace*. He is the former director of an inner city addiction clinic and is a world championship boxing judge. He writes a judging column for www.boxingscene.com, contributes regularly to Westchester Magazine. He founded a boxing program for people with disabilities called, *The Undisputed Champions* and teaches human services courses at Hudson Valley Community College. He lives with his wife, two basset hounds, a bloodhound and three cats in Albany, New York.

Follow Tom and Subscribe to updates at
TomSchreck.com

# BOOKS BY TOM SCHRECK

### The Duffy Dombrowski Mysteries

*On the Ropes*

*TKO*

*Out Cold*

*The Vegas Knockout*

*The Ten Count*

*The Comeback*

*The Shuffle*

*The Real Deal*

*The Split Decision*

*Getting Dunn*

*Redeeming Trace*